If You Could
Be Mine

If You Could Be Mine

by

SARA FARIZAN

ALGONQUIN   2013

Published by
Algonquin Young Readers
an imprint of Algonquin Books of Chapel Hill
P.O. Box 2225
Chapel Hill, NC 27514

a division of
Workman Publishing
225 Varick Street
New York, New York 10014

LIBRARY OF CONGRESS CATALOGING-IN-PUBLICATION DATA
Farizan, Sara.
If you could be mine : a novel / Sara Farizan.—First edition.
    pages cm
Summary: In Iran, where homosexuality is punishable by death,
seventeen-year-olds Sahar and Nasrin love each other in secret until
Nasrin's parents announce their daughter's arranged marriage and
Sahar proposes a drastic solution.
ISBN 978-1-61620-251-4
[1. Lesbians—Fiction.   2. Love—Fiction.   3. Best friends—Fiction.
4. Friendship—Fiction.   5. Iran—Fiction.]   I. Title.
PZ7.F179 If 2013
[Fic]—dc23   2013008931

10 9 8 7 6 5 4 3 2 1
First Edition

To my parents, for always loving me as I am.

If You Could
Be Mine

1

NASRIN PULLED MY HAIR when I told her I didn't want to play with her dolls. I wanted to play football with the neighborhood boys. Even though sometimes they wouldn't let me because I was a girl, they couldn't deny my speed or the fact that I scored a goal on the biggest kid in the yard. Nasrin pulled my hair and said, "Sahar, you will play with me because you belong to me. Only me." That was when I fell in love with her.

We were six. We didn't wear head scarves then. We were little girls, not "whores of Babylon," to be met by the scrutinizing eye of any asshole with a beard. Nasrin has the longest, darkest hair but it never gets tangled or neglected under her *roosari* like mine does. I always think there's no point in making my hair look decent if I have to cover it in school, but Nasrin is always taming her locks — blow drying, using mousse, a flat iron sometimes. No matter what she does to her hair, she will always be the most beautiful woman I have ever seen.

It's difficult, hiding my feelings for her. Tehran isn't exactly safe for two girls in love with each other. I wonder if people can tell I love her when I look at her — in the park, at the bazaar shopping for bras, everywhere. How can I not stare? Even at age six, I wanted to marry her. I told my mother when I came home after playing with Nasrin, who lived a few houses down from our apartment. Maman smiled and said I couldn't marry Nasrin because it was *haraam,* a sin, but we could always be best friends. Maman told me not to talk again about wanting to marry Nasrin, but it was all I thought about.

I thought about marrying her when we were ten and Nasrin cried that I got my period before she did. I thought about marrying Nasrin when she taught me how to put on eye-liner when we were both thirteen. I thought about marrying Nasrin when we finally kissed, on the mouth, like Julia Roberts and Richard Gere did in *Pretty Woman*. It's a stupid movie, but Nasrin always makes me watch it with her. We got the DVD from my older cousin, Ali. He's in university and knows everything cool but gets awful grades. I don't like that the movie is dubbed; the voices never match the actor's lips. And Julia Roberts has big lips. She could fit a whole *kabob barg* in her mouth if she wanted to. It was three months ago that Nasrin and I kissed. Even though I'm seventeen now, it made me feel like I was six again and she was pulling my hair.

We are always around each other, so I don't think anyone will suspect that Nasrin and I are in love. She worries, though, all the time. I tell her no one will know, that I will protect her, but when we kiss I can feel her tense. She keeps thinking about the two boys who were hung years ago in Mashhad. They were hung after being accused of raping a thirteen-year-old boy, but most people think the two were lovers who got caught. I remember the video of the hanging my cousin Ali downloaded for me. I don't know how Ali gets away with the things he does, and would never ask, either. When I saw the video, I wasn't scared, but I got angry. They were so young, just sixteen and eighteen, blindfolded, standing next to each other in the square with nooses around their necks. I felt my neck itch as they were slowly raised on cranes. Whatever crime they committed, I didn't want a part of it. I wanted to stop loving Nasrin, but how do you stop doing something you know you are supposed to do?

Nasrin keeps telling me, "We aren't gay, we are just in love." I've never even thought about being gay; all I know is I love Nasrin more than anyone. Nasrin always used to giggle with the neighborhood girls about boys, but I never joined in. Why should I care if Hassan grew a mustache that looked like a baby caterpillar? It wasn't going to change the fact that I am in love with my best friend. It wasn't going to make my *baba* stop crying, wishing that my *maman* didn't die all those years ago. It wasn't going to change the fact that I had to teach myself to cook meals, and my *khoresht*s will never be as good as Maman's, even though Baba says they are delicious. I miss her sometimes, but these days I just resent her for not being here.

I've gotten used to Baba's long periods of silence. Sometimes he won't speak for two days, but when he comes out of whatever trance he's in, he is in a good mood and pretends nothing happened. I'm no doctor, but I think he is depressed. I wish he would snap out of it.

Nasrin is in my room, painting her fingernails while I pretend to do my science homework. I've been studying a lot for the Concours, which determines which university you get to go to and in what field. About one and a half million students take the exam every year in June, and only 150,000 get acceptable scores. Your performance on the exam is all that matters. Your grade-point average is meaningless, which Nasrin always reminds me when I get a less than perfect score on an Islamic Studies quiz. It's September now and I already feel anxious. I want to go to Tehran University to study medicine, which is just about every student's dream, but I think I actually have a chance. Nasrin on the other hand . . .

"You're staring again," Nasrin says. She looks up from her nails and gives me a smile. I look down at my textbook and hope my face isn't red, like all the other times Nasrin catches me watching her.

"Don't you have homework?" I ask.

Nasrin just blows on her nails and rolls her eyes. "I'm not a genius like you, Sahar. I'm going to move to India and be a Bollywood actress." She stands up and goes into one of her Indian dance routines. Nasrin is an excellent dancer and gets a group of girls together from her school to practice. They usually have me film them while they dance Persian, Arabic, or whatever other dance routines they have been working on. My favorite was when they did the Ne-Yo dance. Black American singers sound better than anything, though I fear saying that in front of Nasrin because she loves her Persian pop so much.

If she spent as much time on her studies as she did her dancing, maybe we could end up at the same university, but I know that isn't going to happen. Now that we are getting older, we have only a few more years left like this together. Things will change. Nasrin will have a lot of suitors. The men will line up on her block. All of the well-to-do in Tehran will come to her family's house, dressed in their best suits.

The suitors will have tea with Nasrin's parents, and they will explain that they can provide her a good life with whatever important and boring job they have. Her parents will pick the best man for her, meaning the one with the most money. Nasrin comes from a good family, and they have money themselves, so she will marry the best that there is. I am not the best. I am an awkward girl with breasts so big that sometimes I feel I might tip over. I don't know when I am going to lose her, but it's going to happen, and I don't know if I will be able to handle it.

Nasrin finishes her dance, and her face falls when she sees mine.

"What's wrong, Sahar *joon*?" she says. She's always been able to read me, even when she doesn't want to.

"I wish we could stay in this room forever," I say. She grins.

"Wouldn't you miss fresh air? The sun on your face?"

"The morality police complaining that your head scarf isn't on properly?" I always go by the rules, but Nasrin couldn't care less. She's always pushing the boundaries, with most of her hair showing at all times and a little scarf flopped over the end of her ponytail. Nasrin sits down next to me and takes my hand.

"We can't live in here forever. There's never anything to eat in your room, anyway." We both laugh, and she plays with my hair.

"I want to marry you," I say, and Nasrin looks at me with a sad expression that makes me feel helpless and pathetic.

"I know you do, *azizam*. We've talked about this,"

"We could run away!" I beg of her. I'd go wherever she wanted.

"We would get as far as Karaj and then what? Sahar, be serious."

I'm not as well off as Nasrin's family, so I couldn't provide for her, or even buy her a bus ticket to Turkey. When I'm a rich doctor, I'll buy her all the things she has grown accustomed to. Maybe until then I'll just lock her up in a shack in a village so no man will ever have her. I'll have sheep guard her, bleating at whoever approaches. Knowing Nasrin, she will probably be choreographing dance numbers with the sheep and putting a video of it on the Web.

"I'll find a way for us to be together." I look her in the eye to let her know I mean it.

She bites her lower lip, as she's done since she was little, and gently pulls at my hair. "We're together now, Sahar. Let's not waste time on what can't be."

What can't be . . . Sometimes I get so angry I want to take off my *roosari* and run into the streets like a madwoman, my hair flying behind me, waiting for Nasrin to pull at it. I see how Ali is with his boyfriends — they're very sweet together, but they are always hiding. Ali is perpetually dating someone new, but he treats the men like they are toys that he is eventually going to grow tired of. Ali introduces his gentlemen to me as his boyfriends, but usually the boyfriends look nervous and laugh like Ali is crazy. They say they are in Ali's class, but I know Ali has never cared much about schoolwork, and I'm pretty sure Ali is planning on studying anatomy when they come over. He's an engineering major.

I haven't told Ali about Nasrin and me. Though Ali told

me he was gay, we never really discuss it. I remember Maman telling me not to talk about it. So I don't. Ali, though, he treats it like it isn't a big deal when he's with me, which I don't understand. In public everything is secret, of course. I don't even know where he finds his boyfriends. A part of me doesn't want to know. I don't want to know what would happen if Ali got caught. It would kill my aunt and uncle in Tabriz, who send Ali lots of money for his "school" when Ali lounges about, smoking *shisha* and playing backgammon. There are things I don't understand about Ali, but I like that he didn't look at me with sad eyes when my mother died. He treated me like he always had, nudging me with his hip and giving me a wink.

I think about telling Ali about Nasrin because it's getting so difficult not to talk about how I feel. I want to shout how much I love her to anyone who will listen, but sometimes I feel stupid even saying "I love you" to Nasrin. I know she loves me, but once in a while I can't believe she could feel that way about *me*. I think that she just might not want to hurt my feelings.

"Maybe when I get into university we can get an apartment," I say, and Nasrin raises one eyebrow. I know. It was a stupid idea.

"You think my parents are going to let me move out of their house? Before I'm married?"

"You'd be living with me. I would keep the boys away," I say with a grin. She leans in closer to me. Her perfume smells like jasmine and vanilla. She's so cruel. I could die from it. Her mouth is close to my ear, and I think she knows how deliciously evil she's being.

"If my parents knew what a devil you are, they'd lock me in Evin Prison for lust." She says it with levity and I smile, but it very well could be a reality. Though I can't imagine Nasrin's parents putting her in any danger. They have spoiled her since birth because she is the baby of the family, with two older brothers. Her parents have always been very sweet to me, but I worry they are nice to me so I will marry Dariush, Nasrin's oldest brother. A family like Nasrin's would typically seek out other wealthy families to marry into, but Dariush doesn't have many prospects. He was suicidal a few years ago over a girl who wouldn't marry him. The girl's father said Dariush wasn't good enough for her because he's a mechanic. Nasrin's parents, Mr. and Mrs. Mehdi, have not produced children who have met their expectations.

Mr. Mehdi is a prominent exporter of pistachios to foreign

countries and it is fair to say that he is nuts about nuts. His wife comes from oil money generated during the Shah's time, though they will never admit it. They were hoping their children would be captains of industry or cancer-curing doctors. But their children had everything handed to them — happy birthdays, nice clothes, and the latest toys — so they had no incentive to try at anything.

Cyrus, the middle one, is hoping to take over his father's business and isn't lazy, but he isn't very bright. Dariush is a free spirit, more interested in learning how to play Cat Stevens songs on his guitar than making a living. Nasrin's only goal in recent years has been to acquire as many shoes as possible.

To Mr. and Mrs. Mehdi, I am the dream child they always wanted and also the example they set for their children. I study hard, I take care of my father, I cook and clean. I'm polite when Nasrin is sometimes too cavalier. When they compare Nasrin and me it isn't fair, and sometimes I think Nasrin resents me for it. We don't ever discuss it. If they knew about the relationship Nasrin and I have, I don't know if they would be more disappointed with me or their own daughter.

I tuck a strand of hair behind Nasrin's ear. She smiles and kisses my nose. I hate when she does that. She knows I do, she's just being tough on me today for all of my wishful thinking. I wonder whether Nasrin would be open about us if we didn't live in Iran. She might be just as scared but for different reasons. She's always been the loud one, but she's scared of stupid things. Things like spiders, the dentist, or not having the latest jacket. She squeezes my hand when she's scared, and lately my hand feels like it is going through early arthritis.

I lean in and kiss Nasrin on her lips. She returns the kiss with urgency, and I definitely know that no man or woman can ever make me feel the way she does. If that makes me gay, so be it.

Sometimes when Nasrin and I kiss, Ayatollah Khomeini's and Ayatollah Khamenei's faces pop into my head. When I was little, I used to think they were the same person, because their names sound the same, they wear the same outfit — a cleric's robe and a turban — and both with long gray beards. Khomeini, now deceased, became the Supreme Leader after the revolution. I hadn't even been born then, but apparently Iran was a lot different. There was a king and girls could wear miniskirts, which is all Nasrin cares to know about that era because it sounds glamorous. In school, they teach us that

Khomeini brought justice and the will of God to the people and how much better the country is flourishing than under the Shah. I'm not sure how much I believe that.

The ayatollahs' photos are everywhere. At the shopping mall, in small businesses, restaurants, parks, on the autobahn . . . and when I kiss Nasrin I feel like they are watching me. I don't know if it's to give citizens a sense of pride or to scare us from questioning our government. I think Khomeini is my "Angry Grandpa," and Khamenei, the Supreme Leader of today, is my "Disappointed Grandpa." Whenever I think of Nasrin in public or at school, I feel their eyes on me. Angry Grandpa is the most judgmental. His brow is furrowed as if to say he knows exactly what I am: a degenerate.

Ayatollah Khomeini has been dead thirty years, but it's as though he never left. He's always mentioned in news broadcasts. Khamenei speaks of him with great reverence during his national addresses, and he's depicted as the father of the country. People typically hold their tongues if they don't agree with that sentiment. Those who don't . . . Well, it makes their life a lot harder. There's a national holiday to commemorate his death. Some people make the pilgrimage from far, far away to visit his tomb and get one free meal given to visitors that day. Most people in Tehran try to get out of town and go visit the Caspian Sea.

Nasrin puts her tongue in my mouth and it makes me forget about Angry Grandpa for a moment. Her fingers run through my tangled hair, and I kiss her neck, making sure I don't leave a mark. We're always so careful, and being that way is exhausting, but we don't know anything else. We hear a knock at the door, and the two of us jump away from each other.

"Yes?" I say in my best calm voice while Nasrin looks into one of her books for the first time all afternoon.

"Sahar *joon,* would you and Nasrin like some *chai*?" my father asks from the other side of the door. This is his way of asking for tea for himself, but it's sweet that he thinks to offer, even though we both know I'm the best at brewing it to a rich, dark color. He puts in too many leaves or not enough. Baba is a terrible cook but a good man.

"I'll come and make some, Baba!" Nasrin is packing up her purse. I hate when she leaves. It feels like a wrestler is squeezing my lungs. "Do you have to go?" I know the answer.

"I have to go home sometime. Don't worry. I might come back, *if* I feel like it," she says with a mischievous smile. I worry that one day she might not feel like coming back. It's the thing I fear most. More than prison, more than the police, more than Baba kicking me out, and more than not getting into medical school. If I lost Nasrin, I wouldn't know what to do with myself. She puts on her head scarf, loose and stylish like she has no respect for the law, and kisses me on the cheek.

"Why aren't you a man, Sahar?" she asks seriously. I shrug, and she turns to leave. I look in my mirror to make sure my cheeks aren't too flushed before I go to serve Baba dinner. He never notices, but one can never be too careful. I'm always careful.

In the kitchen Baba sits at the table and watches me with a vacant expression as I put the kettle on and fill a plate with leftovers. I put the food in the oven and sit in front of Baba, waiting for everything to heat up. He smiles at me, but it's always the same sad expression. I remind him of Maman, and his heart breaks over and over and over. He says that I have the same big, expressive eyes that Maman had.

"When did you get so big, Sahar?" Baba asks quietly.

I want to say, "While you were sleeping through life," but I don't. My father is a carpenter and works on construction sites, mostly making furniture. When Maman was alive, he made the most beautiful pieces. Hope chests for a bride on her wedding day, chairs and tables that the well-to-do would commission. His pieces always have some imperfection now.

"I'm not so big, Baba. You're still taller than I am."

Baba smiles and runs his hand through his gray hair. He got old so fast. Mr. Mehdi looks like he hasn't aged since Nasrin and I were little, but Baba looks like he could be my grandfather.

"You're studying very hard?" He knows I am. It's just that we don't have much else to talk about.

"Yes. I wish the test would just come already so I would know my future," I say, already nervous about the math portion that waits for me in June.

His knowing look makes me suddenly shy. "No one knows the future," Baba says. "Anyone who thinks they do is mistaken. Remember that, my love."

We sit in silence for a minute before I decide to set the table. Sometimes I feel like I should set a place for Maman, because her presence is everywhere.

I feel guilty that I wish it wasn't.

2

Mrs. Mehdi invited my father and me to dinner, and when I asked Nasrin all week what that was about, she wouldn't say. She changed the topic immediately. It's impossible to get Nasrin to share anything when she doesn't want to. She's hiding something from me. She's never done that before.

Baba has on his best suit. He looks handsome for an old man. I've asked him to talk to Mr. Mehdi about sports, since Mr. Mehdi hates any mention of politics. Baba doesn't really talk about anything, but I make sure he will stick with sports exclusively.

I'm wearing my hot pink dress under my manteau, a thin frock that makes sure my bare arms are covered and that my ankles don't show. The pink dress is Nasrin's favorite, so I don't mind, but I hate wearing high heels. I don't know who invented high heels, but that person should be maimed with goat shears in the square. It was probably a man. My dress has a V-neck showing enough of my chest that I'm not so stuffy but not so much that I'm perceived as a loose woman. The plunging necklines on Nasrin's dresses can make her seem loose, which makes me uncomfortable. A bad reputation can be deadly.

When I ring the doorbell, it doesn't take long for Mrs. Mehdi to open the gate and welcome us with open arms. "Nasrin! Our favorites are here!" she yells, and hugs me. She's squeezing really tight, which means she's excited. I bought Mrs. Mehdi apricot-colored alstroemeria, symbolizing friendship and devotion, but the flowers look like they are starting to wilt.

"*Salam, Mehdi khanum,*" Baba says with the utmost formality.

When Mrs. Mehdi lets go of me, she leads us into her home. Most people in Tehran live in newer apartment buildings, but the Mehdis have this old house. It's very Persian, with large columns and a pointed doorway like you would see in a mosque, but the inside is very Western, with all modern furniture. The Mehdis even have a pool, surrounded by a few cherry trees. I would never leave this house.

When we enter the living room, everyone stands up, and I smile at Dariush and Cyrus. I look for Nasrin but can't find her. Mr. Mehdi nods warmly at me. Many of Nasrin's uncles, cousins, and extended family are here. There are others I don't recognize, but I am sure they are friends of Mr. Mehdi.

Soraya, the Mehdis' servant, takes the flowers I brought and offers tea to my father and me. There's alcohol on a nearby table, Efes beer from Turkey and vodka. The Mehdis have always smuggled alcohol in, but I have never asked Nasrin how. My father and I decline the tea, but I smile at Soraya in appreciation. She is now in her sixties, and her daughter, Sima, who is about Dariush's age, goes to Tehran University, much to the Mehdis' chagrin. Sima was raised on the same estate as their children but was expected to grow up to be a servant, like her mother. I always admired Sima and her studying, and we got along. Nasrin used to get jealous, which on some strange level pleased me.

Soraya and Sima are from Afghanistan, and Soraya has an accent that people sometimes make fun of at parties, but I never do. My dad has a slight Turkish accent since he's from Tabriz, and it doesn't embarrass me even though kids sometimes make fun of the Tabrizi accent. I say hello to Soraya, and she smiles broadly. Even though three of her teeth are missing, it's one of the most beautiful smiles I've seen, not counting Nasrin's.

Mr. Mehdi is acting hyper and looking for something. "Where is that girl?" he asks his wife.

"She's still getting ready. Sahar, can you get her from the bathroom?" Mrs. Mehdi asks me, and I nod in compliance.

I go directly to the bathroom and knock on the door. "Nasrin? It's me." She doesn't answer, and I jiggle the handle.

"I'm sorry," she says weakly.

"Sorry for what? Let me in." I'm starting to worry. After what feels like an eternity, Nasrin opens the door. She is biting her lower lip, and she reaches for me, to squeeze my hands. Whatever is worrying her, it must be bad. She turns on her blow dryer, for the noise. We're in for a private conversation.

"Sahar . . . You'll always love me, right?"

"Of course. I always have, why should that change?"

"Everything is going to change. Tonight." I look at her with curiosity, and she wipes at her eyes. "I don't love him. Know that."

Don't love him. *Him.*

Who is she talking about? Why would everything change? The way she's looking at me, so sad and hopeless. There's a ring on her finger. Why is there a . . . Oh no. Oh no, no, no. My face crumples, and I fall to my knees, putting my arms around her waist.

"But you're too young! You haven't finished high school yet!" I sob and feel her fingers in my hair.

"It's been decided." She tries to lift me up, but I am not leaving the ground. If I stand up, if I can stand up, it makes everything real. This isn't real. This isn't real. "Sahar, get up. We have to get out there."

"We were supposed to have more time! You were supposed to give me more time . . ." She tries to pull me up again, and I let her. Everyone at the party will wonder where we are. She wipes my eyes and turns us both to the mirror. We wash our faces, and she carefully dabs at her eyes so she won't spoil her makeup — but everyone will be able to tell we were both crying. We will have to pretend that they are tears of joy. That will be hard for me. Nasrin has always been the better actress. We stare at each other in the mirror. When the bride and groom get married, they sit in front of a mirror, looking at each other as a couple. This is the closest we will get to doing that.

"He's a good man. I trust him. He makes sense." What she doesn't say is: "We don't make sense."

"I can't do this," I say.

"You have to. You're my best friend. You have to look happy."

I know what she means. I have to act my part. Otherwise, it will look suspicious.

"How long have you known about this? How could you agree to it?"

"Stop! I don't have time for this now. Please."

God, we were supposed to have more time.

"I feel like I'm going to throw up," I say.

"Just play happy for an hour. I'll tell my mother you aren't feeling well." She turns off the blow-dryer.

I take a deep breath and look her in the eye. I lean in and kiss her, hoping that it will change her mind. Hoping this whole thing is a dream and a kiss will wake us up like Sleeping Beauty times two. When we pull away for breath, our foreheads pressed together, we're still listening to the hum of the crowd outside. She rushes to the door and walks out, her shoulders back, head held high, and a smile on her face. I follow moments later.

When I reenter the living room, Mr. Mehdi has his arms around a handsome, tall man. His thick hair is jet black, and he wears a navy blue custom-fitted European-cut suit as though he were born in it. He has kind eyes, strong wrists with a Rolex on one, and broad shoulders that Nasrin can lean on. I hate him.

"This handsome young doctor will be the newest addition to our family!" Mr. Mehdi announces. "He has asked for Nasrin's hand, and she has accepted!"

The crowd erupts in cheers, and a feral cry no one hears leaves my mouth. I watch people approach the happy couple, kissing both of them on their cheeks, wishing them well with many children. I catch Soraya's eyes, and she approaches. I ask for a glass of vodka and soda. She offers it, and I drink it quickly, placing the glass back on the tray. The vodka burns going down. She laughs, and I pat her shoulder.

I make my way to the couple, the way everyone expects me to.

Nasrin beams at me. I could slap her. Her smile is so artificial. Her fiancé doesn't even notice, because he doesn't know her the way I do.

"Reza, this is my best friend in the whole universe."

I look at the man next to her, and he regards me with great affection. He must be in his early thirties, and I want to call him a pedophile. But Nasrin is eighteen—younger girls have gotten married.

"The famous Sahar! You are all Nasrin can talk about!" Reza exclaims.

For once I am glad men aren't supposed to touch women outside their family. If he ever hugged me, I would knee him in his sheep balls. I shouldn't think that. It's rude. I think about it again. Though doing so gives me no comfort.

"Well, you are certainly a surprise!" I inform Reza. I can see Nasrin's smile falter.

"Well, we wanted to keep things secret. I didn't know if she would agree when I first came to visit a month ago," Reza says. She met him a month ago! She didn't tell me? I could scream. He looks at her with love, and she just stares at me with a big, stupid grin.

I bet Angry Grandpa would laugh in my face. Disappointed Grandpa would just tell me to go pray. I grab Nasrin's shoulders and kiss her sloppily on both cheeks. I hug her and whisper in her ear.

"He's very handsome." I say it with venom, and I feel her stiffen. When I back away, I look up at him. He's so tall. "I'll let you two deal with the mob."

Reza chuckles. I feel Nasrin's eyes on me, but I turn around and look for my father. I tell him I will be in the bathroom.

In the bathroom I spot the Western-style gold-colored toilet the Mehdis insist on having instead of the squat toilet installed in the floor of most homes. I throw up in it. Twice.

3

My bed is the only place where I feel safe. After school I come home every day and lie here, thinking about the engagement party. It was a week ago, maybe two — I've lost track of time. Only when the call to prayer sounds from neighboring mosques do I know time has passed. Nasrin was so calm about everything. Does she even care about what happens to me? And to us? I was just something to keep her busy until the Superman of suitors came forward. He is so handsome, and *tall*. I'm short and only just learned how to make my one eyebrow into two. He is a prince, and I am a frog. A hairy frog that is due for an eyebrow wax and breast reduction, with a sexual orientation that will get this frog imprisoned sooner or later.

I go to a different school than Nasrin, which is a blessing because I have no interest in seeing her or her friends at school.

Nasrin attends a school where a lot of rich families send their children. I go to a high school that takes only students who do well on the entrance exam. It's hard to get in, you have to be smart. Money can't buy you a place at a special school — or at a university, for that matter. Nasrin's friends at school are probably cooing over her, asking what kind of dress she will have. Nasrin will love the attention, showing off her ring in between math problems she needs help solving. I don't feel betrayed by her. I just don't know how I am supposed to move forward. There is a knock on my door.

"Baba, I'm still not feeling well," I say.

"God, you sound depressed! Let me in!" Ali calls.

"The door is open," I mutter.

Ali makes a grand entrance, holding plastic shopping bags in the air like he is Haji Firooz bringing gifts on our New Year's.

"Sahar *joon*! It's been too long."

I get up and kiss Ali on both cheeks. He takes my arms and gives me a look up and down. "You look awful." He's right. I slump back down on my bed, and he quirks an eyebrow at me. He notices the framed photograph of Nasrin and me on the floor by my bed.

The photograph was taken when we were both four. My *maman* took the photograph on the Mehdis' property. When Maman used to look at the photograph, she would comment on how much Nasrin and I looked like Mrs. Mehdi and her. Our mothers were childhood friends, both from wealthy families. They went to school together, attended the same parties, did practically everything in tandem. After the revolution Maman's family's wealth diminished. Her family was still well off, but Maman's brother inherited most of the money, and Maman was expected to marry an affluent suitor. The problem was that she picked Baba, who was not what her family had envisioned. Ali's father reaped the benefits of Maman's disappointing choice and kept the family money, telling Maman she had found a husband to provide for her.

I wonder what life would be like if Maman had received her share of the family wealth. For one thing Nasrin and I would probably be going to the same school. The curriculum at my school is rigorous. Nasrin's school just makes sure the students pass. Maybe it wouldn't be so bad that I was in love with her if I had money. I could buy Nasrin away from her parents.

Ali picks up the frame and regards the photograph with a

smirk. "You two, always together," he says. "It's kind of nause-ating." Ali puts the framed photo on my dresser and looks at it again. "I heard she's getting married. Leaving you alone." His eyes meet mine, and I am trying to figure out what he knows.

"When I'm a doctor I can find my own groom," I say, and he grins the way he always does when he knows more than he is saying. He opens up the plastic bag and tosses me a DVD. There is a woman on the cover, sitting on top of a building with heart shapes around her. Ali has been selling DVDs, CDs, and other banned items. He doesn't need the money, but it keeps him popular in certain circles. The DVDs for sale in stores are censored and have to be deemed appropriate. Nasrin and I watched a legal copy of *Lost* once, and all the bodies had been digitally covered in black. Where there were supposed to be scantily clad men and women, everyone had computer-imposed black sleeves and pants. It's too bad. I would have liked to see Evangeline Lilly in a bikini.

"Watch that when your father isn't around." Ali chuckles and sits down on the bed next to me.

"What's it about?"

"A love story. It's good. It has subtitles because no one would dub it." If no one would dub it, that means the

American Persians don't approve of this movie, either. It must be—no, it couldn't be. He wouldn't.

"*Hamjensbazi?* Gay stuff?" I ask, and Ali looks at me with sympathy.

"Sahar, it takes one to know one."

I stand up and hurl the DVD to the floor. "You're wrong! I'm not like you! Going to your cafés and parties! What you do is wrong, and I am *not* like you. You think everything is a game, but it isn't. What happens if the secret police or guard finds this trash on you? You never think about any consequences."

Ali doesn't look bothered. He looks at me like I am clueless. He picks up the DVD and places it on the dresser next to the photo of Nasrin and me.

"I just thought you needed to talk to someone. I know this isn't much of a life we have here, but we still have to live it."

We still have to live it. Even when Nasrin is gone, we still have to live it. My face contorts in ways I can't control, and Ali wraps his arms around me. The spurts and gasps begin. I let everything out and I think about my mother, how she told me when I was six to ignore my desire to marry Nasrin. Even if Maman were alive, I couldn't talk to her about Nasrin.

When my sobs subside, I back away from Ali's chest. His

shirt looks like a used tissue. He must love me because even though clothes are important to him, he doesn't seem to mind.

"I'm sorry about your shirt," I say as I wipe my eyes.

"*Eshkal nadare*—it doesn't matter. I need to go shopping soon, anyway."

I sit back on the bed, and Ali continues to stand. I need him to know that I'm still not really like him. I don't drink or do drugs. I think his haircuts are sometimes stupid, and I don't want to live a secret life. I just want to be like everyone else and have a home with the person I love.

"Does it show? I mean, how long have you thought that I—"

"I can tell from how Nasrin looks at you sometimes. Like you're a kabob she wants to bite into."

"You're disgusting." I laugh. If Nasrin has looked at me that way, I have never noticed. I've always felt that I'm the one who's been so swept up in her, but I guess Ali sees something I don't.

"She's not the only girl in the universe," he says. No. But she's the only girl in *my* universe. He wouldn't understand. He has never been in love. "Come by my place Friday. I'm having some people over."

"I don't know."

"Oh, it will be tame. I'm not going to throw you to the lions right away." Friday is my day off from school, and Nasrin and I have always spent it together. I have other friends, but they're schoolmates. I can't talk to them about how I'm really feeling, not the way I could with Nasrin. Last Friday I stayed in my room all day. Nasrin called, but I couldn't make myself talk to her. Baba answered the phone and told her I was studying. I know I can't do that again, or Baba might get suspicious. That is, if he's paying attention. So I could use a distraction, and a part of me is curious about Ali's world. I've seen glimpses and heard his stories, but to be in it would be something else. Plus it would be something I can brag about to Nasrin.

"I'm scared," I say as Ali looks out the window at the busy street below. I'm not sure what he finds so interesting. The view is always the same as the day before: traffic that never slows down or stops for pedestrians, diesel fuel pumping at a relentless pace out of the Peugeots, the motorcycles that look like they might disassemble at any moment, the occasional Mercedes or BMWs that make little kids jump up and down pointing. There's always the same Afghani boy, organizing garbage from barrels and piling it on a cart he wheels around in the street, never on the sidewalk. Old men stand in front of the corner shop as though they are guarding the cigarettes and gum with their lives, but they're really there for the shade from the nearby trees.

Ali squints at something. "I always envied those stupid pigeons," he says. "They can leave whenever they want. Maybe that's why I stomp on them when I can."

I'm still thinking about Ali's party. "I can't go to your apartment alone," I say. If I walk somewhere by myself, it's more likely I'll be stopped by the guard, especially at night-time. There's no way I am going to ask Baba to walk me to Ali's place. Even Baba won't believe that I'm going over there to study. I'm scared, but I need to get out of this room. I need to find ways to distract the gnawing pain that feeds off of every surface of my body.

Ali looks at me and grins. His mask is back in place. "Oh, don't worry your pretty head. I will send someone to get you. Someone even your Baba would approve of." He ruffles my wild, curly hair and I swat at his hand. "What's for dinner tonight?"

The rice I have cooked is hard, and Baba and Ali don't say

33

anything at the dinner table, but I can see their jaws overworking. I would have done a better job if I hadn't been thinking about Nasrin. Baba looks thinner than usual, and I know it's because I haven't really been cooking much of anything. If I don't remind him to eat, he won't. His heart isn't in it. I look at my plate. The meat is rare, mixed with the cooked carrots and prunes. Not my best try at this dish. We should have ordered pizza.

Ali pokes at his plate and looks around the kitchen, probably wondering why he decided to invite himself over.

"So, *Dayi,* how is work?" Ali is desperate for topics of conversation. He never likes to discuss work, even other people's. These days Baba goes to a workshop he used to own but had to sell because he didn't produce enough to keep it after Maman died. Whatever he manages to build, he will sell to merchants at the bazaar, mostly merchants who owe him favors from the old days. The favors will one day run out. How many dressers or hope chests can any store need, especially when the Chinese can make them for less? I hope I can take care of him by the time that day arrives.

Baba considers Ali's question as he drinks his Coca-Cola. "Good," he says at last, and we return to silent eating.

I smell Maman's cigarette smoke in the air around us. It happens from time to time. I know it's impossible, but I do smell it. Ali claps his hands and pulls me back from my morose thoughts.

Baba keeps chewing.

"Sahar's getting such good scores, *Dayi*!" Ali exclaims. "She showed me all her perfect scores. You must be very proud."

"Yes. Sahar is my highest achievement," Baba says. From the little life left in his eyes gazing at me, I know he means it.

"And because she's doing so well, she and her girlfriends want to go to the movies this Friday to celebrate. Sahar says she's afraid to ask you, because she doesn't want to leave you alone for dinner." I throw Ali a worried glance. I can't believe he has the gall to lie to Baba this way. Then again, it would be kind of nice to not be so goddamn well-behaved all the time.

Baba takes another long sip of his soda and looks at me.

"It is just girls?"

If he only knew that it's the girls he should worry about.

"*Baleh,* Baba. Just girls," I say, and Ali concentrates on his plate, all innocence, as though he isn't planning on corrupting his younger cousin. He's a devil.

"That's fine. Just don't come home too late. You need an escort home, though."

I can't have Baba pick me up. I'll have to take a taxi. I look at Ali and he smirks at me. Now that it's decided, a feeling of dread settles in my stomach.

4

My escort to Ali's party should be arriving at any minute. I check Baba's eggplant stew one more time. He will like it, or he should, because I have spent all day making it. I turn the heat off and leave it on the stove. I check my appearance in the hallway mirror for the thirtieth time. This whole scenario is crazy, but it's exciting to go to a party with older people. Knowing Ali, they all will probably have cool jackets or the latest sneakers. Hopefully they won't notice my worn-out Adidas and faded jeans.

My reflection greets me once again, and I groan. All this makeup has turned me into a sad prostitute. I should have learned how to apply it a long time ago, but Nasrin usually helps me. Wiping at my cheeks, I hear the buzzer. I hurry to the front of the apartment to push the button, feeling a little scared about who will answer.

"Baleh?"

"Salam, I'm Ali's friend Parveen. Are you ready?" She sounds nice. Her voice is sweet but not syrupy or artificial. I grab my coat and head scarf and put them on quickly. I exit the apartment, locking the door behind me, and try not to rush down the stairs.

Parveen is waiting for me beyond the gate at the bottom of the stairs. She's wearing the trendiest trench coat — muted blue instead of the typical beige, black, or dark green — and flawless makeup. Her eyes are an unusual green. The front of her hair peeks out from behind her *roosari,* black, sleek, and soft looking. She is radiant and not who I was expecting to pick me up. I thought Ali would send someone who looked like a depressed schoolmistress as an omen of what I would become if I didn't come to this party.

"You're gorgeous! Just as Ali described you," Parveen says, and I blush, even though she is just being nice. We kiss each other on both cheeks, and she takes the lead as we walk to the bus.

We stand at the back of the bus with the rest of the women.

The men stay in front. This way if the bus gets crowded, the men and women don't brush against one another inappropriately. It's a blessing, really. The last thing I need is an old man's pencil penis brushing against my bum on his way to the mosque.

Parveen asks me the usual questions: what I am studying, if I have seen the latest Islamic Republic–approved movie in the theaters. As I answer, I feel all the eyes on her. A young man with an Armani T-shirt gives Parveen a wink. I don't think she notices. If that man had winked at Nasrin, she would have noticed and giggled about it. Then she would kiss me in the privacy of my room, saying things like, "You're the only one for me. I just like the attention." Sometimes I wonder if Nasrin keeps me around just to stroke her ego.

We get off of the bus and walk side by side. Ali's apartment is near Vali-Asr, a nice neighborhood that a university student should not be able to afford. Two men on a motorcycle whiz by us on the sidewalk. I clutch my purse. There have been a lot of robberies courtesy of motorcyclists ripping bags out of pedestrians' hands. The two men don't try to steal from us, but they almost crash into a fruit stand because they are checking out Parveen.

Parveen's hair is peeking out slightly, and she doesn't wear the heavy makeup that most girls do. She doesn't have trendy tattooed eyebrows, either. Some girls shave off their eyebrows and then have these hideous cartoonlike brush strokes tattooed over their eyes. The makeup and the tattoos are all because the face is so important. Girls can't lure boys with cleavage or tight jeans, so all the effort goes into the face. Parveen seems to know she doesn't need all that. What's most attractive about her is the way she walks, confidently but with a very feminine stride. Her hips sway in a way that Angry Grandpa would definitely disapprove of.

"I'm glad you're coming to the party. It will be so nice to have more girls there," Parveen says, and she seems genuine.

"I'm a little nervous," I say. "I know how Ali is, so I can only imagine what his friends are like."

Parveen laughs loudly and unapologetically.

"Oh, everyone is nice. Crazy and a little messed up, but nice. If anyone's mean to you or too insane, just come find me." She winks at me. It is dusk, and I am glad it is getting darker so Parveen won't notice my face is scarlet red. I know she is not flirting with me—that isn't the impression I get. I wonder: if Nasrin saw us walking together, would she be jealous?

"You're quiet! Are you sure you're related to Ali?" Parveen asks. She nudges me.

I recall when I first met Ali. My parents and I drove up to Tabriz for a holiday weekend. Maman and my uncle finally made amends about the inheritance, but I think they did so in hopes of not isolating me from her only family. Ali was thirteen and nerdy, with glasses. I was eight and thought he was so cool, dancing to boy bands from the USA in his parents' luxury condo. Sometimes I wish we could go back to that time when my biggest problem was learning all of the Backstreet Boys American names to impress Ali.

When we reach the tall apartment complex with a fountain in the front, encircled by meticulously pruned shrubbery, Parveen rings Ali's buzzer. Moments pass. Parveen hits the buzzer again. "God, he's probably loaded already," she says with a hint of disapproval. The intercom crackles.

"Yeah?" a gruff voice—definitely not Ali's—barks. Maybe this was a bad idea. Parveen rolls her eyes and winks at me.

"The pigeons fly free," she says in a lilting, ever so soft voice.

The buzzer goes off and Parveen opens the door for me. We enter a lobby and she pushes the elevator button. When

I follow her into the elevator, I try not to notice the sway her hips make when she walks. I hate that I notice. A nice girl wouldn't notice. We stand side by side, waiting to get to the twelfth floor, the top floor. Her perfume is delicious, but I prefer jasmine and vanilla. Nasrin's scent . . . I'm so pathetic.

"Don't be scared," Parveen says right before the elevator door opens and we exit to the right. I can already hear the music from the other end of the hall, and I wonder how Ali gets away with all this. Parveen knocks on the door, five times and with a particular rhythm. Code. The door opens a crack, and a behemoth of a man peers at us, sees Parveen, and opens the door.

"Farshad, you take your job too seriously," Parveen says as she enters.

Farshad reaches for her coat, but Parveen keeps her chic head scarf on. "This is the package I picked up," she says, nodding in my direction. Farshad has an eighteen o'clock shadow. He looks like an Olympic wrestler, with a neck so thick he could wear a car tire as a choker. Farshad extends his hand, blocking me, and I wonder what it is I did wrong. Parveen begins unbuttoning my coat, and it dawns on me that Farshad is the doorman. I undo the rest of the buttons and remove my head scarf. Farshad accepts them and whispers into Parveen's ear. She blushes and swats him away, then links her arm in mine as we mill through the throng of characters.

The air is laced with heavy smoke, a blend of cigarettes and something sweeter, which I know Baba would not approve of. A thick bass with a techno accordion thrums in the background. There are men everywhere. Most of them have stupid faux hawks that everyone thinks are cool, even though they look like rooster combs. Some skinny boys wear *tight* jeans. Their hair is long and shaped haphazardly, with intentional cowlicks and too long in the back. Some wear lip gloss and eyeliner as though doing so is perfectly natural. A fat man wears a blond wig, which makes perfect sense with his red, sequined dress. I don't belong here.

Ali's apartment is furnished with white leather couches on a white tile floor, which is silly, because white is more likely to get dirty. Ali probably didn't think that through. The huge flat-screen television plays Persian music videos, set on mute and beamed in via illegal satellite, and I'm pretty sure the coffee table is made of granite. Granite! Parveen clutches my hand in hers and leads me through the labyrinth of aftershave scents, nipples, and once hairy arms now waxed smooth. A

43

man who must be in his forties, with a badly dyed beard, boldly eyes Parveen, and she adjusts her scarf to fit her head more securely.

Parveen yells over the music to me. "It's as though they have no respect for a lady."

I wouldn't have guessed Parveen would be so modest. Some women always wear head scarves in mixed company. The very religious ones look like black tents, with only their faces peering out from the folds of the *chador*. Covering my head has always made me feel foolish, but I respect a woman's decision to cover up so long as it's *the woman's* decision. It shouldn't be a decision for a man or a government to make.

The apartment is big, two bedrooms, and with all these people, it takes a long time to push through. We reach Ali on his throne, a couch in the back of the living room. Young men surround him, some lying down on the floor and another seated on the armrest. If only they had known him when he had those thick coke-bottle glasses. I wonder if they'd be interested to hear about the magic tricks he used to practice for hours.

"Parveen! You brought the guest of honor!" Ali says. He claps his hands in delight before standing up and hugging me close. His breath smells like whiskey. The onlookers stare at me with curiosity, and I have never felt more scrutinized or more popular in my life.

"Everyone," Ali addresses the crowd, "my beautiful cousin, Sahar. Make her feel welcome . . . or else." Blushing, I push a little away from Ali. The smell of alcohol is overwhelming.

"Stop embarrassing her," Parveen says quietly, suddenly shy. The energy has shifted, somehow. It's because of Ali. Parveen is definitely barking up the wrong tree. Ali grins at her, clearly clued in to the huge crush she has on him. I hope I'm not that obvious when I look at Nasrin.

"Thank you for bringing her, Parveen," Ali says. "You're a sweet girl." Parveen blushes and glides over to some dancing boys. Ali hollers at a young man pouring drinks and points in my direction. I shouldn't drink. Baba wouldn't like that. It's not ladylike. Ali looks me up and down and raises his eyebrows. "You look good, kid. Nasrin help pick out your outfit?" My shoulders slump. I was doing so well.

"No. She didn't," I say, looking around the room for a distraction.

The dancers are in full swing. Their hips undulate with calculated precision. Some of the masculine men shake their shoulders while the more feminine ones curve their arms in slow, languid movements. Ali puts his arm around my shoulders, and a young man wearing mascara with pockmarks on his face delivers my drink in a glass shaped like a woman.

"Here, it shouldn't be too strong." Not wanting to be rude I take a small sip. I immediately spit it back into the cup. It's disgusting. "Oh, come on!" Ali says as he takes my cup. "There's hardly anything in there." He takes a swig and burps.

"How can you drink that?" I ask, not in disgust but awe.

"Lots of practice." He gives the drink to a guy with long hair and a T-shirt with Madonna's face on it. "Listen, I'm sorry I brought up Nasrin."

"It's okay. She's not dead, she's just getting married."

"What's the difference?" Ali says, and I chuckle a little. He leads me to the dance floor. I hate dancing. All the attention and feigned sexiness isn't for me. I shake my head, but Ali won't have it. He grabs hold of my hips and moves them side to side. I feel like a metronome. He releases me and flings his arms around wildly. How is he so free to do whatever he wants? Trying not to make too much of a fool of myself, I think about how Nasrin dances. She sways slowly, back and forth, and adds a little shoulder shrugging but not so much that she seems like a harlot.

For a while I actually don't feel so out of place, and other than a few men dressed as women, the party is fairly "normal." Well, aside from the water pipe full of opium that three gaunt men are smoking in the corner. They all sit on a rug on the floor, and I wonder if Ali is going to be livid when they spill ashes on it.

Parveen is dancing in my periphery, and soon we are having a dance-off. When her shoulders come forward, mine shrug back. I look around at my surroundings and notice no one cares how anyone looks, dances, or what they are able to do with their hips one way or another. Parveen shakes her hips like a belly dancer, and that's when I know she's won. We laugh, and I resign in a comic bow of defeat while Parveen continues to dance.

Ali joins me and walks me over to the makeshift bar, an out-of-place circular, plastic picnic table. He pours me orange juice. Whatever liquor was intended for my drink he pours into his own. We tap our plastic cups together and survey the wonderful mess that is his apartment.

"How do you get away with it? I mean, don't you worry about the police?" I ask. He makes a farting noise with his mouth.

"We have an arrangement. Besides whatever guards do show up, we pay them off. Everyone has a price." He nods in Farshad's direction and whispers in my ear, "He's on the police force. I throw him a pretty young man every once in a while. Don't worry yourself about these things, Sahar. Just have fun."

I preferred Ali when he was nerdy, with glasses. He wasn't so smug then. I look around the room, and though I am sure about some, I can't tell about others — can't tell if they're like me.

"Is everyone here, um . . . you know?" I ask.

"Does it matter?"

No. It doesn't. I notice Parveen on the dance floor having a great time. She isn't gay. Of this I am sure. "Parveen likes you a lot. Too bad she isn't your type." I kid Ali, but wouldn't it be easier if he just married her? They wouldn't have to hide all the time. He isn't looking for the great love of his life, and this way he wouldn't be lonely. She's a nice girl and she cares about him. Maybe she can cook. It could work, couldn't it?

"No, she's not my type. Though I guess when she was Ahmad, we would have had a shot."

"Sorry?"

"Parveen. She used to be Ahmad." I still don't get it. I blink at Ali a few times. "Don't be so square, Sahar. Parveen's a transsexual."

I look over at Parveen again and try to find anything remotely masculine about her. Ali notices my staring.

"Look at her hands. It's the one thing he left her."

I see now that they are larger than I thought when she held my hand in hers. Her knuckles are broad and her thumbs are thick.

"But she's . . . I mean, how —"

"Sahar, it's okay. She helps other people like her. They aren't doing anything wrong. Besides, if the great Islamic Republic says it's a legal medical condition, then by Allah they must be right." Ali punctuates his sarcasm with a dramatic salute. Trying my best not to stare at Parveen, I take a long sip of my orange juice.

"So, everybody knows? Is she going to get in trouble?" Ali shakes his head.

"Like I said, it's legal. The government even helps pay for the surgery."

"But why?"

"Because they are trying to fix us." He says it with indifference, but I cringe.

Fix us. That includes *me.*

I'm starting to feel sick. This whole party was a terrible idea.

"I have to go home. It's getting late," I say. Ali raises his eyebrows.

"I'll have a car here for you in no time." He pulls out his mobile and walks to the bathroom, the only quiet part of the apartment.

Parveen makes her way over to me. I try my best not to act differently from when I first met her.

"You stopped dancing!" she says. "You were doing so well."

"Yeah, I'm not feeling too great. I asked Ali to call me a taxi. This isn't my usual Friday night." It's the most honest thing I have said all evening. She puts her arm around me and my shoulders stiffen. *Please don't notice.*

"Ali's parties can be a little much. This was actually pretty tame compared to the others. He attracts some odd company, heroin addicts and that kind of thing." Ali knows some real winners.

"Oh," I manage to reply. Parveen's arm loosens, and I hope it isn't because she knows how uncomfortable I am.

"It's just most of the people here, we don't have many op-portunities to express ourselves. It can be hard, hiding all the time." Yes. It can be. She beams at me, and I do my best to smile back. She's been so nice all evening. I hate that I keep looking for clues that she was once a man.

"Here, Sahar, give me your mobile." I hand it over, and she types in her number. I don't know why. I doubt I will call her. Especially after I have embarrassed myself. "It was great meeting you," Parveen says. "My number, if you want to hang out again. Something nice, like coffee. No crazy stuff." Our thumbs brush when she hands me my phone, and there he is. I take the mobile back and thank him.

Her. I thank *her.* Damn it.

Ali comes over and whisks me away. Farshad hands me my coat and head scarf. I put both of them on quickly, giving Parveen one last glance. She smiles and I feel terrible.

"Did you have fun?" Ali asks when we descend in the elevator.

"It was different." I never felt more uncomfortable in my life, you look messy, and I don't think I know you like I thought I did if you throw wild parties with a cop as your doorman. But other than that, it was a fantastic evening.

Ali and I exit the building to find a Mercedes-Benz parked in the driveway out front. He saunters over to the driver's window and taps on the glass. The window lowers and reveals two women with Louis Vuitton head scarves. Glamorous.

"Hello, Mom, Daughter," Ali says. The woman behind the wheel looks to be in her late thirties. The girl in the passenger seat looks younger than I do. The girl extends her hand, which Ali kisses. I look around to see if anyone notices. Not that Ali cares. Public affection between the sexes is forbidden. So are Facebook, dancing in public, and women in football stadiums.

"Is this the package?" The older woman asks. I really wish everyone would stop referring to me as that. Probably just Ali wanting to pretend he's a gangster.

"Sahar is my cousin and very important. Now, no stops until she gets home. You promise?"

"Of course, Ali. A ladies' agreement."

"Cute." Ali smirks and opens the back door for me. "You did pretty well, kid. You still have to loosen up a little more." I roll my eyes and he laughs. I enter the car and the door closes.

Ali leans into the window to address the girl in the passenger seat.

"Britney Spears for you, *khanum*." He hands her a bootleg CD, and her eyes double in size.

"Merci, Ali Agha!" Agha? Since when do people call him "Sir"? Ali winks at her and taps the car. He is done with us. The older woman closes the window and drives out of the driveway. The girl turns around in her seat to talk to me. If I thought I had hooker makeup on earlier, this girl makes me look like a mullah's wife.

"Salam! Do you like Britney Spears?"

"Um, sure," I say, and she puts the CD in the player. Daughter says some words from the song, but they sound funny coming from her mouth. Even though she's speaking in English, you can tell she's from Iran. Mom in the driver's seat is focused on the road, her mouth drawn tight and her eyes darting to the side window every so often. Her daughter bounces happily to the music, and I do my best to keep quiet. Something about Mom's focus makes me nervous. What is she looking for?

Daughter turns around to me again. "What grade are you in?" she asks.

"Last year of high school," I say. "What grade are you in?"

"I don't go to school anymore," she says with a sad smile.

"Listen to your music," Mom says in a stern tone. Daughter shrugs and turns around to face the front. I should have stayed at the party. When we reach a red light, Mom makes eye contact with a man about forty in a Peugeot next to us. She lowers her window. The man tosses a crumpled piece of paper into the car, and Mom immediately closes the window. She hands the crumpled paper to Daughter, and Daughter takes out her mobile, unfolds the paper, and dials the number scrawled on it.

We continue driving and stop again at another red light. Mom takes the phone from Daughter.

"Baleh?" Mom asks in a sweet voice. I look to the right and see Peugeot man leer directly at us. Something about this feels very, very wrong. Daughter lowers the volume, her spirits dwindling along with it.

"No, the one in the back isn't mine. Just the one in the front," Mom continues. This can't be happening. "Seven hundred thousand toman. That's the price, take it or leave it." When the light turns green, Mom hangs up the phone and curses under her breath. Daughter tries to hide how pleased she is. Sweat forms at my hairline, and I wish I could take off this damned head scarf. Daughter turns up the volume on her music, and Mom deftly maneuvers around other cars. Almost home, almost home, I'm almost home.

Daughter turns around again. "You look kind of sick," she says. Mom smirks.

"I'm fine. Thank you," I answer brightly. Let's pretend I didn't see or hear anything. Daughter touches my hand and I look up at her eyes.

"What's your favorite subject at school?" she asks in a way that gives me the impression people don't speak with her often.

"Science. Do you like science?"

"No. But I always liked literature. I was pretty good."

"You're very smart! Literature is my worst subject." It isn't really, but she looks so elated, I am willing to lie as much as she needs me to. She turns to Mom.

"See, Boss? I'm smart!" I do my best not to throw myself out of the moving car. Almost home, almost home. I'm almost home.

"Yes, child, you're smart," Mom says, her jaw clenched and her eyes narrowly focused. We reach my apartment building, and I fling myself out of the car the moment Mom stops. I slam the door in my haste, and Mom lowers the window.

"Thank you both. Very much," I say with as much restraint

and calm as I can. Daughter waves with enthusiasm, and I wave back. Mom nods and raises the window. When the silver Mercedes drives away, I rush into the apartment building. I run all the way up the stairs and unlock the apartment door. Baba sits on a couch watching the news.

"Fun evening?"

"Uh-huh."

"Did Nasrin go with you?" That's when it occurs to me. I haven't thought about her in the past twenty minutes. I will have to call and thank Ali in the morning.

"No. She didn't."

5

IT IS TIME I face the music. If I don't show up to see Nasrin, people will start to talk. Baba will ask questions. But being here doesn't mean I have to like it. Soraya opens the door to the Mehdis' home. She bows her head slightly. I should be bowing to her—she's my elder, after all. Instead I forgo formality altogether and kiss Soraya on both cheeks. She looks so happy and surprised that I think I should have started doing this a long time ago, in place of our formal nods.

I take off my coat and head scarf and hang them on a nearby coatrack. I've tried my best to look attractive. I don't know if it will work. Maybe if Nasrin sees me look my best, she will call off the wedding. The possibility of that happening is about the same as a chance of a mullah's admitting to watching *Baywatch* via illegal satellite.

I walk into the living room, where Dariush strums his guitar, legs up on the couch like he's the king of the castle. I clear my throat to make my presence known, but he continues to strum without looking up at me.

"Hi, Sahar." He chuckles, still strumming. "The ladies of the palace aren't home yet." I sit down on a chair and listen to him play. "Do you know this song?" he asks.

"No."

"Cat Stevens." He starts singing in broken English, and I wish he would just play without the added vocals. He sounds so stupid. My grin is waning. I should probably go and come back later. Dariush stops warbling and plays with smooth strokes, not making any eye contact with me, very much in his own world. The Mehdis' talk of our getting together is pure wishful thinking. Dariush is no more interested than I am.

"Can you believe this wedding is happening?" he asks. No, I can't. It makes me nauseous and I want to punch Nasrin's fiancé in the face with an audience of men dressed as women rooting for me.

"I'm happy for Nasrin," I say. I have been rehearsing that line in my bathroom for two weeks, checking the mirror to make sure that I look sincere when I recite it.

"I don't see her as a wife," Dariush says. "She'll probably take Soraya with her to cook Reza's meals and sew buttons on his shirts."

"I am sure she will be a good wife." I do mean that. Nasrin loves attention, but I think Reza will dote on her and she in turn will be good to him. Reza seems the type to be bossed around . . . the lucky horse's ass.

"Marriage is a farce," Dariush says with a determined tone. Who knows how long he's been reciting *that* in a mirror? I remember when he would talk to Nasrin and me about the girl he was going to propose to. He always went on and on about how gorgeous she was, an angel among mortals . . . blah, blah, blah. Once the girl's father denied Dariush's proposal, he went on about how she wasn't even that pretty, a devil clouding his better judgment. Dariush, like Nasrin, inherited the spoiled rotten gene.

"You've always been smart not to be interested in boys," he says, and I try my best to continue breathing. Am I that transparent?

"Sorry?"

"I mean, it's good that you studied. You won't need to get married. So you can put on airs at parties? No, you're on the right track, Sahar." He is congratulating me on my one day being an old maid. What a charming fellow.

"I'm happy for Nasrin." This time it sounds even more rehearsed than the first time, but Dariush doesn't notice or let on as he plays another song. Soraya enters the room with a tray of tea, a cup for Dariush and one for me.

"Soraya, you don't have to do that," Dariush says. He stands up to grab the tray from his servant. Dariush was different when he was younger. He loved being waited on hand and foot, as though he was entitled. Since he's been working as a mechanic — and after being rebuffed by his would-be fiancé — Dariush likes to play at being blue collar when it's convenient. He has just traded in one version of pretension for another. He plops the tray on the table and waits for me to pour for the two of us. Soraya exits quietly. I look forward to the day when her daughter can get her out of here.

I hand Dariush his tea. He takes a sugar cube in his mouth and bites down on it, drinking his tea around the sugar cube, which intercepts the liquid before it goes down his throat. He used to mimic the Europeans and stir dissolved sugar into his teacup. Now, it seems, he prefers to drink tea like his own people. Dariush is such a lout. I shouldn't think that. He's not such a bad person; he just has some growing up to do. I hear the front door open and then slam, followed by the sounds of Nasrin and her mother arguing. It isn't clear what they are arguing about, but I don't care. I'm excited and nervous to see Nasrin again.

Mrs. Mehdi enters first, calling for Soraya to take the shopping bags out of her hands. Mrs. Mehdi sees me and Dariush and her eyes brighten immediately.

"Oh, look at you two! Having tea together!"

I immediately put my cup down before she gets any more ideas. If she thinks I am going to spend my life serving tea to her lazy son while he strums the same three songs over and over again, she is horribly mistaken. Soraya rushes to her mistress and takes the bags from her hands.

"Soraya, bring out some pastries for everyone," Mrs. Mehdi commands, still eyeing her oblivious son and me. She walks to me and I stand up, hugging her. Over her shoulder comes a vision. It is Nasrin in a strapless red-velvet dress that hugs her in all the right places. Our eyes trap each other. Nasrin doesn't look happy to see me. Or rather, she's trying not to, but her eyes always betray her. I stiffen in Mrs. Mehdi's grasp. She lets go of me, and I pull my eyes away from Nasrin, maybe a millisecond too late. Mrs. Mehdi smiles at me, but there's something behind the smile I can't place. I muster the biggest smile I can as my mind races. *I have no lustful, passionate, raging feelings for your daughter. Not a one. Can't you tell by my overcompensating grin?*

Mrs. Mehdi turns her head to address Nasrin, and I relax, a little.

"The bride to be and I went dress shopping. She insists on breaking them all in. It's going to get wrinkled!" Nasrin rolls her eyes at her mother's complains. I do my best not to drool.

"What do you need so many dresses for? Don't you just get married in the one?" Dariush asks in an unkind tone.

"For parties, my son," Mrs. Mehdi explains. "Stop slouching," she adds as she walks over to him and sits down. "Sahar, we haven't seen you in ages! I hope you haven't been avoiding us."

"No! No, of course not," I stammer. Nasrin smirks. "I've been busy studying, and I assumed you would all be busy getting ready for the wedding."

"They're making this wedding such a big deal. What a waste." Dariush is interrupted by his mother shushing him.

"Sahar's just jealous." It's the first thing Nasrin has said, and I look at her with a bit of fear. "She's jealous that I'm getting married and she's not."

"Nasrin! Be polite!" Mrs. Mehdi says. Everyone is just so assured of my future as an old maid. Do I reek of homeliness or lesbian? Nasrin exits the living room, and I don't run after her right away.

"That girl! Forgive her, Sahar. She's been under a lot of stress lately," Mrs. Mehdi says.

"I can imagine." I assumed Nasrin would go along with everything and be happy about all the attention she is getting. She's getting what she wants, isn't she? The kept life, a doctor husband who is good-looking. And her parents will finally love her the way she wants to be loved. She will have a wonderful life.

"Can you go talk to her, Sahar?" Mrs. Mehdi pleads. "She's been in such a bad mood lately." I nod and try my best to take slow steps to Nasrin's room instead of sprinting like an Olympian. Loud music pours from her room; it's one of our standard methods for masking our conversations—and other activities.

I knock on Nasrin's door and she opens it. She grabs my arm and pulls me in, then slams the door shut and throws me against it, locking it from the inside. She crashes her lips urgently to mine. This is the most passionate I have ever seen her. My eyes open in shock as I take her in. Her teeth are bared and her tongue begs my mouth for entrance. I close my eyes and allow her in. Her hands are grabbing my neck, and I don't know if she might choke me. I don't care. If there's a way to die, this should be it. When I hear her moan I push at her shoulders. She stops for breath, panting and looking at me with predatory eyes.

"Where the hell have you been?" She lunges forward, merging our mouths together in such a feral, animalistic way that I push her shoulders more forcefully.

"Stop! Stop it," I whisper. She looks at me with confusion and annoyance, a wild tiger hunting the next meal, smelling blood in the air. "What about him?" I can't say his name. I'm amazed I'm even thinking of *him* at all, but she is marrying him. We both breathe heavily, and she shrugs.

"What about him?" Nasrin says it with such indifference, I almost think she doesn't know whom I am referring to. I gape at her and she grunts in frustration.

"You're getting married! Or have you forgotten?"

"Oh, shut up, Sahar." She backs away from me and slumps

onto her bed. We stare at each other, each waiting for the other's next move. She asks, "Where have you been?"

"I'm sorry I haven't come to see you."

"It's been over two weeks!" She says it with desperation I have never seen from her before. She's been counting the days. I am thrilled.

"I thought it would be better . . . It might be easier for us, if I didn't see you for a while," I say.

"For someone who is supposed to be so clever, you are such an idiot," Nasrin says and I can't believe it, but she's crying. Her mascara is about to run, her cheeks are flushed . . . and is that snot? I walk over to her bed and sit down next to her. She wipes at her eyes and curses herself under her breath. Throughout our friendship, Nasrin has always been the cool one, slightly aloof, even indifferent at times. That I followed her around like an idiot . . . Well, it was embarrassing sometimes, but that's just the way it always has been. This is different.

"You're getting married. What did you think was going to happen?" I ask.

"I didn't think you'd leave! That's not the plan!" There is a plan? The only plan ever mentioned was my scheme to run away to some remote village.

"But you're going to be his wife."

"So?"

"So, kissing me—that's cheating, isn't it?"

Nasrin looks at me like I am the biggest fool in the universe. She puts her hand over mine and grips it. "I don't care about him. I need him, but I want you."

I have to remind myself to breathe, because it isn't often that Nasrin voices her feelings. Especially concerning me. Nasrin takes her other hand and wraps it in my hair, tugging me toward her lips, and I hungrily accept. It means so much just to hear her say what I never expected her to.

Only, she's choosing him anyway.

I stop responding to her kiss and she looks at me in confusion.

"Nasrin, this isn't normal."

"I know it isn't. Believe me, I wish I didn't have these feelings for you."

"No. I mean, doing this when you are engaged to someone else."

"He doesn't ever have to know! Why are you making this an ordeal?"

I always knew she was selfish. At birthday parties she always got the biggest icing flower on the cake. When we went to the movies, the popcorn was always in her lap. We always listened to the music she liked. We would spend only half an hour at the museum I wanted to go to before she complained about being tired.

"You want me to continue this?" I ask her, not sure what I want her answer to be.

"Yes. Don't you?"

This has been the plan all along. *Her* plan. Have her perfect marriage and string me along for the ride. I rip my hand away from hers and touch my bruised lips.

"What about me? Did you ever think about me?" Of course she didn't.

She folds her arms in front of her and quirks an eyebrow.

"Come on, Sahar. We can be just as we've always been."

A secret. I'm supposed to wait for her in the shadows. When she's done feeding him dinner and performed her marital duties in their bed, I'm supposed to come over and comfort her. Tell her how beautiful she is. Worship her in private when he gets her all the time. I'm a lap dog. How long has she seen me this way?

"You're cruel, Nasrin." I stand up and walk to the door, but she yells out my name.

"Sahar! What did you expect? I'm not going to be anything other than someone's wife! It's what my mother has been grooming me for. How was I supposed to be anything other than what she wants me to be?"

"We could have talked about it before you decided to go through with it!"

"This was always going to happen, Sahar. What could you have done to change it?"

What could I have done to change it? There's nothing I can do. I have no resources, no plan of attack. I'm just a girl. A girl. If only I were a man. A man with a hairy face who could slouch his shoulders if he wanted to and walk around with short sleeves in the hot sun. If only . . .

"How many months until the wedding?" I ask her.

"Three. Why?" I kiss her with ferocity, and this time it is she who is struck dumb.

"I'm going to find a way." I make sure she understands that I am serious. I can tell that I am scaring her a little bit, but she kisses me and it is all the confirmation I need.

6

I DON'T KNOW IF Parveen will come to see me today. My text message to her was sincere, and she agreed to meet me, but there's always the possibility she won't come. I haven't planned everything out, but if there's any way I can be with Nasrin, I will do whatever it takes. I sip from my soda cup. I couldn't think of a place to meet other than Max Burger. I'm sitting in the upstairs area with the kids' playroom. Two small boys play in the ball pit, and I hope they don't suffocate in red plastic.

At a nearby table two little girls are showing their mother the DVD that came with their kid's meals. It's usually a high-quality cartoon bootleg. Nasrin sometimes orders the kid's meal just for the movie. Her favorite is *Toy Story*. The movies are in English, so I do my best to translate for Nasrin. She never wears her glasses to read the subtitles, but it hardly matters. My English isn't the best, but Nasrin knows about as much English as she does Japanese.

"*Salam,* Sahar *joon*," Parveen says just as a red ball flies from the pit to hit me in the head. One of the small boys looks apologetic while the other one laughs. Parveen smiles, but more at my expression than because the ball hit me. She takes a seat across from me. She looks gorgeous, but I still feel embarrassed and have trouble looking her in the eye.

"Thank you for meeting me," I say. Parveen keeps her hands under the table, and for that I am grateful, though she doesn't do it for my benefit.

"I'm glad to see you again, Sahar. We didn't get much of a chance to talk at the party." There's a silence, and since I am the one who initiated our meeting, I really should speak. I rehearsed what I wanted to say, but now that I'm facing her, the words aren't coming.

"Would you like a hamburger?" I ask, and she looks amused.

"I have to watch my girlish figure. And for some reason I don't think you came here to eat," she says. I avoid eye contact and look back to the two girls and their mother, eating their hamburgers.

"Well, Ali told me that, um . . . that you, uh, were at one

time . . . What I mean to say is that it's really cool about . . . you know, things that have taken place and that you are . . . um, that you—"

"That I'm transsexual." I gape at her and how easily she says it. What if someone heard us? Isn't she afraid?

"Yes. That."

"I assumed you found out. You were distant toward me at the end of the party."

I feel terrible.

"Ali told me."

She nods and looks a little deflated. "He shouldn't have done that. It's private. I mean, I'm proud of who I am, but I don't announce it to everyone I meet." I sense that she is as disappointed it was Ali who thoughtlessly shared her secret as she is that I found out. I should ruin another one of his shirts just to teach him a lesson. Parveen adjusts her head scarf, even though it hasn't shifted since she sat down. It's as though she is reminding everyone around her that she is indeed supposed to be wearing one. She's a woman, and so she is entitled to the same oppressive dress code as the rest of us.

"I'm sorry if I reacted poorly. You're just the first person I met who, um, well . . . you know," I say, now working hard to

71

maintain eye contact. I need her to trust me if I am going to ask for her help.

"You're not the first person to react the way you did. Some people have reacted much worse," she says as she discreetly raises one of her sleeves. I see two circular scars, the diameter of a cigarette on her arms. "I made the mistake of not being up front with a boyfriend. He wasn't the gentleman I thought he was."

Before I can stop myself I rub two fingers over one of the scars. I know it was the right thing to do because her arm relaxes. I meet her gaze, and she leans her head to one side, assessing my intentions.

"He was stupid." It isn't the most articulate thing I could say, and it probably shows I am very much seventeen, but she smiles, and I think maybe this whole thing might not turn out as badly as I feared. I withdraw my hand from her arm and she pulls down her sleeve.

"It's fine. He has a very fat and ugly wife now."

I laugh and she chuckles lightly. I hope we can be friends. It feels nice to laugh again. I sense that it may be too soon, though, to start throwing questions at her about her change from male to female.

"That party was crazy," I say sheepishly. I am sure she is used to crazier nights, especially if she is close with Ali.

"I usually don't go," she says. "I'm not crazy about associating with those kinds of people." I suppose she means the party animal, druggie types.

"Ali had these two women drive me home. A mother and daughter."

Her eyes widen in horror.

"He didn't! Oh, those two — they are always so careless about everything." She explains that they aren't actually mother and daughter, but it's easier to conceal their business if they pretend to be.

I nod as though I knew that already, but only because I don't want to seem naive about absolutely everything. Since the night the supposed mother-daughter duo dropped me off, I look for their car everywhere I go. I just want to make sure the daughter is okay. I didn't even learn her name, but something about her has stayed with me. I've even been carrying a little book of Persian poetry in my bag to give to her if our paths cross again.

Parveen and I discuss everyday things. She works at a bank but didn't let them know that she is trans because she is afraid the bank might fire her. She explains she is lucky that she passes. She asks about school and what I plan to study. When I talk about our dissection lab in biology, she looks squeamish, so I cut it short and explain that I am interested in being a surgeon. She says she owes her life to her surgeon because she was desperately tired of being trapped in the wrong body.

"How long did you feel that way?"

"Since I was very little. I always felt uncomfortable. I used to dress in girls' clothes and then I felt at ease. My parents didn't mind in the beginning. They found it funny. It was only when I wanted to leave the house in girls' clothes that they got nervous." It reminds me of when I told Maman I wanted to marry Nasrin when I was six. After Maman told me to never bring it up again, I buried the thought deep in my mind, but that never felt right. I wanted to be with Nasrin all the time.

"Did you try to be, like, um . . . I mean, couldn't you just stop?" I know it's a stupid question. I wish I could stop loving Nasrin, but I can't. It must be sort of the same thing for Parveen.

"I had a beard when I was a teenager," she says. "It was so scratchy and terrible."

The mother sitting near us with her daughters abruptly stands, telling her children to get ready to go. She rushes them and doesn't put away their trays. She takes the two girls by the hand and sneers as she makes a hasty exit. My face feels hot, and Parveen shrugs.

"Eavesdropping is unbecoming," Parveen says, loud enough for the woman to hear her. She doesn't seem upset by the woman's reaction. I wonder how often she finds herself in these situations. I wouldn't be so brave, I think. Then again, if I had the girl of my dreams with me, maybe I wouldn't care what anyone said. I finally own up to being hungry, and Parveen laughs and says she has a bit of an appetite, too. We order two combo meals.

Sometimes when I eat hamburgers I pretend I am living in the West. I heard that Europeans treat fast food like gourmet, and Americans just keep getting fatter and fatter. That's probably why Americans always seem so happy. I sometimes pretend I live in Los Angeles. Nasrin's aunt and uncle live there, and they send pictures. They have three cars and it's always sunny. Where they live almost everyone speaks Farsi, and they celebrate New Year's with great pomp and circumstance, like in Tehran. They see American movie stars in supermarkets and get their gas pumped by our exiled pop singers. Nasrin eats that stuff up. It must be nice living somewhere that has all different kinds of people. How do they manage all that diversity?

Parveen takes ladylike bites into her hamburger, and I feel like an impolite buffoon. I am sure I have ketchup all over my mouth. She wipes her mouth with a paper napkin, and her large hand is front and center in my view again, reminding me why I'm here.

"I guess I was curious because I think I'm different," I say, and her eyebrows arch in interest. I'm still not sure I can tell my secret, but I can allude to it. "I feel uncomfortable in my body, too." This isn't untrue. It's just not for the reasons she might assume. Parveen seems to recognize something in me as she again leans her head to one side. I know what it is to be different. And she knows I know.

"Does Ali know about how you feel?" He knows I'm in love with Nasrin. He doesn't know that I am prepared to do whatever it takes to be with her.

"No. I haven't told him," I say. Lying by omission isn't so hard. I should go into politics. "I guess I just want to learn more about—well, about stuff. You know, make informed decisions and things." There is so little time before the wedding.

I don't really have time to decide whether I am making the right decision. Parveen considers me, scrutinizing me to see if I'm being honest. I had better sell this. "I'm desperate. I know, you don't really know me, but I don't know where else to go." My voice wavers and I'm trembling a bit. Parveen's face softens.

"There's a group meeting in three days, if you would like to come. You can see if their stories speak to you." She pulls a pen from her red clutch purse and writes the address and the time of the meeting on a paper napkin. I have to keep reminding myself to be brave. I can do this for Nasrin. I can do this for us. Parveen takes one last bite from her burger, and then plops more than half of it back on her tray. She shoves the tray away in disgust, and her lack of appetite makes me feel fat since I ate all of mine in record time.

"The sacrifices we make to be beautiful." Parveen sighs.

Sacrifices. How many before you get what you want? I should probably go on a diet. Then again, if I go through with this I will probably need to bulk up. I won't be as tall as Nasrin's groom-to-be, but if I gain some muscle maybe I could take him in a fight. Unlikely, but it's a nice dream. Before Parveen and I leave the restaurant, I buy a burger to take home to Baba. I have bigger things on my mind than cooking.

7

I RUN ALL THE way from my school to Nasrin's and stop to catch my breath in front of the gated building. I haven't seen her in a few days. Her house is a zoo, with all the preparations her mother continues to make and Dariush's habitual lounging about the house. He occasionally fixes a car, though it is always for someone who can't afford to pay him on time. Cyrus is usually wearing a suit and follows Mr. Mehdi around like a clueless chicken, pecking at his father's heels when they go to the pistachio factory. I don't want to run into Reza. I may throw up on his shoes. Or confess that I get in heated kissing sessions with his bride-to-be.

I see Nasrin come out of the building with a swarm of girls. She is the only one who has changed out of her school uniform into a casually draped head scarf and a stylish manteau. I'm shocked there are no teachers around to stop her. The other girls surround her like she is royalty, and it is easy to see why. That damn giant diamond on her finger. She never wears it when I come over. All the girls chatter around her, but she doesn't look at any of them. She looks only at me. It is in these moments that all the heartache seems worth it. She smirks and I duck my head, trying to hide my blushing cheeks from her friends.

As soon as her friends see me, they treat me like I am the German ambassador able to give them a visa. Nasrin has informed them how important I am, though without giving them the real reason why. We walk along the sidewalks that line the busy street, and I listen to the girls chatter about bouquets, caterers, and hotel reception halls. Nasrin, in their eyes, has "made" it. Nasrin and I walk in sync with each other, holding hands. It is not uncommon for women to hold hands or for men to hold hands — it's all seen as innocent. Holding someone of the other gender's hand? . . . Well you'd better be married. Two of Nasrin's flock leave, and two more are left with us. These two girls are new to me, and I assume they are fascinated with Nasrin's pending nuptials or just with Nasrin in general. I notice one of them eying her with a look that is a little more than friendly. She's lovesick, poor dear. Do I look like that when I'm around Nasrin? Allah forbid, I hope not.

Because I'm in a Nasrin haze, I don't notice the police car. Two officers get out of the car and head straight for Nasrin.

"Is there a reason your elbows are showing?" the first officer asks, and my heart momentarily stops. It isn't the first time I have seen these confrontations. I don't want them to hurt Nasrin. Her two remaining admirers have run away, and I stand next to Nasrin, looking at her forearms that have three-quarters sleeves. I wish she wasn't such a slave to fashion. Her dark green coat is tight fitting, and she's carelessly let the three-quarter sleeves slip above her elbows. As usual her loose scarf barely covers the back of her head. I would rather her wear an Afghani burqa slathered in garlic juice than be put in danger.

The thing I don't understand about Nasrin is her disregard for consequence. She looks the first officer in the eye, meeting his brooding, predatory gaze, and she plays the complete innocent.

"My clothes shrank in the wash!" she lies. "I didn't have time to change."

I notice the policeman's gun in his holster. He reaches for

his baton and thumps it in his hands. I inch myself in front of Nasrin.

"Sir, her mother is sick, and my friend is terrible when it comes to domestic tasks. She put the dryer on too high," I say in the most desperate of tones. The policeman sneers, clutching his baton in his meaty hand. The larger policeman behind him looks at me. I don't recognize him at first. He is wearing sunglasses and a military hat. But when he folds his arms in front of his chest, I recognize him as Farshad, the bouncer at Ali's party. He recognizes me, too, and his mouth twitches.

"Your friend looks like a whore," he says. It's not uncommon for a policeman to say something like this. I want to rip his eyeballs out of their sockets with my fingernails. The worst scenario would be if Nasrin is arrested. Girls have gone into prison virgins and come out broken. I will be damned if I let that happen to her.

"She isn't very smart, sir," I say. I hear Nasrin harrumph behind me. She shouldn't take it personally. I'm only trying to save her skin. She can be so childish sometimes.

"You are dressed fine, sister," the other policeman says. "You should give your whorish friend some fashion tips."

Although I am terrified, I can't help but also feel offended. Is he calling me homely? I'm in my school uniform, a baggy, dark blue coat that reaches to below my knees and a tight head scarf that lets only my face poke through. Should I have put on some more makeup?

"Normally she is dressed just like I am," I explain. "Her mother is sick and doesn't have time to check her before she leaves the house. We are going straight home and this will never happen again, I swear." The first policeman grips his baton again, and that reminds me of a girl at school who got caught at a party with alcohol. After a conversation with an overzealous officer, two of her fingers were fractured and purple, and both hands were covered in bruises.

"Let me take care of them," Farshad says. His torso is even more imposing in the daytime. I don't know if he's going to help us or hurt us. If Farshad does hurt us, Ali will find out about it, but I don't know the nature of their arrangement. The smaller but more menacing policeman moves aside for Farshad, and he takes both Nasrin and me by one arm. He pushes us into the backseat of his police car and slams the door behind us. Nasrin is in tears, hysterical and yelling my name over and over again. I watch Farshad pat the other policeman on one shoulder, and then the second man smirks and walks into a restaurant.

Bystanders look at us through the window of the police car. Some are sympathetic, while others just enjoy a good show. Nasrin covers her face with her hands and I rub small circles on her back, assuring her everything is going to be okay. Farshad enters the car, buckles up, and starts the engine.

The car is filled with the sounds of Nasrin's hysterics and the police radio. She continues to mutter about what her parents will do to her when they find out. I try to meet Farshad's eyes in the rearview mirror, but he doesn't acknowledge our presence. He is not the easiest person to read.

"Sahar, I'm so scared," Nasrin says as she rests her head on my shoulder. I wrap one arm protectively around her shoulders.

Farshad drives us to a part of the city near Tehran University and stops the car in a side alleyway. He is going to violate us here. He is so big, I won't be able to fight him off of Nasrin. Maybe I can spare her for me, if I have to. Oh, please. Who would take advantage of me when Nasrin is the much prettier target? Farshad turns in his seat and looks at me.

"Turn right on the main street until you see Restaurant

Javan," he says. "Ask for a table and tell the host who you are. Your cousin will be there eventually."

Nasrin looks at me in shock, and I thank Farshad. He nods, turns back around, and waits for us to get out. I scramble out of the car and yank on Nasrin's arm. Her body is limp from shock, and I drag her behind me. When we have cleared the car, Farshad screeches from the alleyway, his exhaust clouding us in shame. We were lucky. Nasrin is catatonic until I pull her into me for a hug.

"Are you okay?" I ask. She pulls away from me suddenly. It's just a hug, you paranoid brat! "Nasrin, until your wedding day can you please wear full-length pants and shirts? Or at least look like a walking tent instead of a sex goddess?"

She laughs in a nervous and exhilarated way, but I find the situation anything but funny. "You're lucky I knew that officer! Don't you know what could have happened?" At last I'm the one who knows what's going on. She needed me today, and that feels good. Her laughter subsides, but she still has a bit of a grin left over, and I do my best not to smack her. Or kiss her.

"You think I look like a sex goddess?" Nasrin is beyond exasperating. I take her roughly by the hand and lead her to the main street that Farshad told us to walk to. I walk fast, dragging Nasrin behind me while I frantically make my way through the crowd, my eyes peeled for Restaurant Javan.

"Since when are you so mysterious?" Nasrin yells at me over the din of the crowd. "I'm supposed to be the exciting one!" Ignoring her babbling, I see the restaurant. Pushing forward, I make my way to the entrance, feeling Nasrin breathing on the back of my neck. The scene at Restaurant Javan is similar to the one at Ali's apartment. The place is packed. Unlike at the party, no one is dancing, but the coiffed hairdos, shaved forearms, and mascara-wearing boys are familiar. Of course Ali will be here later.

"Can I help you?" A short, stocky bald man with a thin mustache looks at us with skepticism. He wears a bright orange suit.

"Can we help *you*?" I hear Nasrin mutter unkindly.

"My name is Sahar Ghazvini. I'm . . . um, Ali is my cousin." Before I can utter another word, his eyebrows rise so high, I'm afraid they might levitate off his face.

"You're the little cousin he goes on and on about! Come in, please, come in." The short man whisks us into the center of the restaurant. I can feel eyes on me, from all directions. Some guests even smile at me in recognition from the party the other night. The short man seats us in a reserved area, a tier above the floor. The tables up here have clean white linen tablecloths, as opposed to the rest of the establishment, where wooden tables are scrunched together, leaving no room for guests to breathe.

I sit down and survey my surroundings. There's no particular decoration or advertising to suggest that this is different from any other restaurant, but the clientele is definitely telling. No one touches anyone else, but all the patrons sit precariously close. One thin man pulls gum from his mouth suggestively and twirls it around while glancing across the way at a chubby tough guy with a collared shirt. The short man who greeted us addresses Nasrin and me again.

"Our kitchen is ready to make you anything you like! Would you like some *joojeh kabob*? Whatever we don't have, we can make it for you." He speaks with nervous excitement, and I am certain Ali has some illicit dealings here. Whether he's selling DVDs, alcohol, or drugs, I imagine this is where Ali makes his headquarters.

"No, thank you, sir," I say. "We will just wait for Ali, if that is all right."

"I'll have an orange juice and some baklava, if you have

any," Nasrin says, and I throw her a stern look. We aren't here to snack! The short man hurries away and yells for his staff while the other guests stare at us, trading not so hushed whispers. Nasrin relaxes in her chair, looking over the menu as though we hadn't been in great peril just moments ago.

She sighs. "I shouldn't really eat too much, since I need to go dress shopping, but I am craving some *zereshk polo*." I can't believe this is what my life has become.

"Nasrin, as soon as Ali comes, we have to get out of here. I don't think it's safe." I look from side to side, hoping no one from my day-to-day life is here.

"Oh, relax, Sahar. We don't even know when Ali will get here. It's still light outside, and Ali is nocturnal." She isn't wrong about that. Ali lives his life mostly in the dark. "Just enjoy. Besides, it will be nice for us to catch up, since you are always either studying or avoiding me."

"I'm not avoiding you. I just feel guilty. When I do see you, I mean." What I really mean and can't say is that when our mouths are crashing together, I feel like Allah is looking down on a cheating sinner who is in way over her head.

Nasrin lowers her menu slowly and raises an eyebrow in a way that can't be interpreted as anything but suggestive. "But

I love our study sessions!" she says, and I feel my face grow hot. "You know I rely on you to educate me." The short man and two waiters come by with plates of dates, baklava, a tray of tea, and orange juice and pomegranate juice. They place the goodies in front of us like we are royalty. Nasrin is used to such treatment and nods at the waiters before she dives right in.

"Sir, really, I don't think we can afford all this," I protest, but he shakes his head.

"Please, it is the least we can do," the man says. "We called your cousin, and he should be here shortly. He's a very special customer. Please enjoy, and don't hesitate to ask for anything else."

Before I can argue he flits away with his servers as though I am Queen Farah. Nasrin shoves a whole piece of baklava into her mouth, ignoring the crumbs that land at the corners of her lips.

"Mmm. Not bad. I wonder where they get their pistachios from."

"Nasrin, we really shouldn't be here."

"Why not? It's not fancy or anything, but their food is adequate." She reaches for another pastry. I see the chubby guy with the collared shirt stretch his arms, not so subtly flexing his muscles. The skinny gum smacker takes notice. All of this is so obvious. They just need a photo outside of two men kissing to let citizens know where to pick up a male date. Except that it's illegal. Just like a girl's stupid elbows showing.

"Do you want some orange juice?" Nasrin asks, and I shake my head. "Well, can I have the pomegranate juice? It's supposed to be good for the skin, and I can't afford to get any pimples." She babbles on about the arguments she's having with her mother over wedding arrangements, oblivious to our surroundings. I think it's for the best that I not alert her to the unusual atmosphere we find ourselves in. She may have a panic attack.

"What is the matter with you, Sahar? You're so jumpy."

"Nasrin, I know you have always lived above everyone else, and now you have your perfect life planned out . . . but wake up! We almost got arrested! Who knows what could have happened to us? You can be so *stupid* sometimes." I wince as soon as the word comes out of my mouth. I have never called Nasrin stupid. It's a sensitive topic for her—she knows people see her as a stupid, beautiful girl. She's actually very clever, but it seems like I'm the only one who knows that.

"I'm sorry. I didn't mean to lose my temper," I apologize.

"Oh, is that what just happened? I'm sorry—I'm just too *stupid* to read emotions." She isn't going to make this easy. Since her engagement, there have been so many cracks in our respective armors. I wonder which of us will crumble first.

"I'm angry because I can't always protect you. I need you to be careful, because if anything happens to you . . ." My voice starts to break.

"Don't cry, Sahar. Shhh, don't do that." She places one hand on top of mine.

I don't often cry in front of her. Nasrin is the crier, especially when some girl is wearing the same dress as her at a party. These days it seems I am the one crying in front of Nasrin, crying over Nasrin, crying about being without Nasrin. I'm so exhausted. I wipe my eyes with my free hand, and she slowly withdraws her own. She gives me a furtive smile, and her eyes gleam. Because of me. No one else gets that look. I feel better.

"Hello, you two dolls! Run into some trouble today?" As Ali walks toward our table, all eyes are on him. His pace is steady and nonchalant; he's used to the lustful glares, the jealous murmurings, and the awed glances. I don't dare ask what business he does here. Nasrin and I stand up to greet Ali, and he kisses each of us on both cheeks, with not a care for prying eyes or for the danger such an action could create.

We all sit down and the short man comes by again, with three waiters this time. Ali asks for two orders each of *kabob soltani* and *zereshk polo,* which he knows is Nasrin's favorite. The waiters hurry away from our table. This is unusual for food service in Iran. Usually the waiters come around when they feel like it, and you may or may not get your food in two weeks. The short man comments on what a lovely young lady I am. Ali treats him like a pimple he is having a difficult time popping. After a few more bows of the head, the man walks away. Ali rolls his eyes at us and doesn't bother to explain why he is so important here.

"Farshad called me. Good thing he was there," Ali says, looking at me with concern. He always cheats the law, but it's funny that the one time I get in trouble he gets upset.

"It's my fault," Nasrin admits. "The officer didn't agree with my being fashionable," I know she would take blame only for me. Everything else she just pins on someone else.

"My cousin seems to get into nothing but trouble because of you," Ali says. "I hope you appreciate her *friendship*." It may be the first time I have ever seen him angry.

"I do appreciate her *friendship,*" Nasrin snaps. "I don't appreciate you insinuating otherwise!" The two of them look at each other like dueling princesses fighting over the last lipstick.

"Well, your husband will be the one to deal with you soon enough. What's his name again? Ramiz? Rasheed?"

I kind of like it that Ali says this, but then I feel guilty. It also reminds me that I am running out of time, because Reza is a lot of things, but insignificant is not one of them. I'm not ready to reveal my half-crazed plan to these two, though.

Nasrin bites back. "At least I have people who care about me. Not like the false friends you push drugs to." But this is not the place to challenge Ali.

"If you two cared about me, you wouldn't land me in dangerous situations all the time," I say. They look at me, their faces softening.

"Well, what fun would it be if we didn't get you in dangerous situations once in a while?" Ali says with a grin. "You'd be so boring, reciting biology notes all the time."

Nasrin chuckles. Fine. If it takes them making fun of me to get along, so be it.

This whole time, Ali has been fiddling with his cell phone. "I've arranged a ride back to your apartment."

"Ali, no! Not them again!" I don't know if Nasrin would be able to handle the "mother-daughter" duo. Ali laughs a little.

"They won't accept any calls while they drive, I promise." I don't have enough for cab fare, and I can't risk Nasrin riding the bus and getting in trouble again. She's covered her elbows, but her sleeves don't reach to her wrists. I nod in compliance. It will be nice to see Daughter again, at least.

"What are you talking about?" Nasrin asks.

"Some girls who work for me. They're in sales," Ali says. I don't know whether I should laugh or be disappointed. When did Ali become this? "They won't be here for a while. Why don't we enjoy some dinner, hmm?" He signals the waiters and they scurry into the kitchen. They come out quickly with steaming plates of saffron rice and chicken with dried mulberries. When a plate of kabob is placed in front of Ali, he grins at me affectionately. I try to do the same back. I'm suddenly not hungry.

"Are you okay?" Nasrin asks. She always knows when I'm upset, or at least when it's convenient for her to notice. Ali chews on a morsel of kabob with the genteel, delicate manners of an aristocrat.

"Sahar does not approve of my livelihood," he states with indifference.

"You don't need to have a livelihood! You're a student," I say through gritted teeth.

Ali looks amused by my out-of-character nerve. "Careful with your tone of voice with me in here. The *others* are watching," he says in a mocking tone. The others. Others like me. He can't even say in public what these people are. What *we* are.

"Why do they treat you so wonderfully here, anyway?" Nasrin asks. Ali looks at her with amusement.

"Nasrin *joon,* these are my people." The way he says it screams both arrogance and pride.

Nasrin shrugs. "So what, you peddle bootleg CDs to this crowd?" She's really testing his patience. I love her for it. He motions to a neighboring table. Two older women sit with each other, and even though they are not touching, the love in their eyes for each other is evident.

"Like looking in a mirror, isn't it?" Ali asks. "Hopefully, you two will age better than those poor souls over there." There's a bit of malice beneath his words. Nasrin looks at the women. Like I said, she is anything but stupid. She glances around the room, and suddenly she sees the knowing glances men are giving one another. Her eyes land on a woman with a prominent Adam's apple.

"Oh my god," she gasps, and Ali laughs. Nasrin's mortified expression upsets me. Those women sitting at that table, looking at each other longingly, are no different than us. Nasrin has no right to be prejudiced. She starts hyperventilating, and I tell her to breathe.

"Oh, you are always so dramatic," Ali tells Nasrin. "I'm surprised you two get along at all."

"Leave her alone," I plead with him. "She's not used to this." I wonder if I ever would have been as ridiculous as Nasrin is being right now. I touch her shoulder, and I don't care what it looks like. "Nasrin, it's okay. We'll go home soon. I tried to tell you earlier, but it's not so bad, is it? No one cares who we are in here." I don't know if that's true. There could be a secret police officer in here, but Ali is so relaxed, I doubt that's an issue. I don't know how Ali does what he does, or even *what* he does, but he's like Iran's gay messiah. I'm not sure if that's an honor or not.

"What do you mean who *we* are?" She's angry.

I let her comment wash over me. She doesn't want to mix with anyone here. She doesn't want to be like anyone here. This evening is full of disappointments. Ali drops his fork with a loud clink and stares at Nasrin with fierce eyes.

"You're a guest here because of Sahar. That is the only reason I am tolerating your backwards thinking."

"It isn't backwards if it's against the law," Nasrin snaps, and I wish I could disintegrate into my seat. Ali slowly leans forward on the table, until he is almost over Nasrin's plate, making direct eye contact.

"In here is my law. Don't forget it." Nasrin cowers under Ali's gaze.

He's right. When he's decided she's uncomfortable enough, he leans back in his chair and picks up his cutlery. He cuts into his kabob and without looking up addresses me.

"Eat up, Sahar. Before it grows cold."

I keep my eyes on Nasrin as her heavy breathing subsides and she takes a sip of juice. For the rest of our meal there is nothing but weighted silence and the occasional sigh. Most of the sighs come from me. Ali's phone rings, and he answers saying, "I will send them out right away." We follow Ali outside, and I nod in thanks to the poorly dressed short man who was so kind. Ali doesn't let us stop to properly thank him. The Mercedes is waiting for us outside, and I face Ali. I want to give him a big hug, but people would misconstrue it.

"Stay out of trouble," Ali says. "I'm the rebel in the family, okay?" The glint in his eye reminds me of Maman.

Ali goes to speak with Mother through the open window of her car, and I turn and whisper to Nasrin. "Let me do the talking in the car," I say, and after all the shocks she's had today, I think she might actually listen to me. I open the car door and let Nasrin in, and then I follow her into the leather backseat. Daughter turns to me, and I notice a bruise under one eye. I try to hide my shudder and do my best not to think about what customer left her a souvenir. She still manages to smile wider than anyone I have ever met.

"*Salam!* It's good to see you again," Daughter says. I beam and hope it's enough to keep her spirits up.

"It's wonderful to see you, too! I have something for you." I reach into my book bag. I can feel Nasrin's eyes on me. I am sure she is jealous and wondering how I know Daughter. I pull the book of poetry from my bag. Before I hand it to Daughter, my eyes meet Mother's sunglasses in the rearview, asking her permission. Mother nods and I give the small book to Daughter.

"It's your favorite subject," I say, and she laughs in delight.

"Oh, thank you! Thank you so much! I'm going to read

everything!" she babbles. "When should I return it to you? If you leave me your address—" I cut her off.

"It's yours. All yours." Something should be. Daughter looks at the book, caressing the laminated cover with her hand. Tears surface in her eyes. Nasrin looks at me with an *Is-she-serious?* face. I don't think Nasrin understands how anyone could get so excited about a book.

Daughter laughs again and shows the book to Mother. "Did you see what she brought me? A book of poems! Isn't it wonderful?"

Mother, looking out onto the road, can't deny Daughter's enthusiasm. The edges of her lips curl up slightly, and it's the most emotion I have yet seen from her. Daughter turns back to Nasrin and me. She regards Nasrin as though she were a new toy.

"Your friend is really beautiful," Daughter says, and I blush. Nasrin straightens her shoulders in self-satisfaction. "Thank you," she says. "You're very pretty yourself. I love your lipstick."

"Do you work, too?" At first I don't understand Daughter's question to Nasrin.

"Work?" Nasrin asks.

Mother turns the wheel and finally speaks: "No. She's not one of us." I am doing my best not to laugh. Maybe Nasrin really could be a sex goddess.

"You'd do really well, I think. Men would put you in high demand," Daughter says before turning back around to face the front. Comprehension washes over Nasrin's face, and her jaw may reach Australia if she isn't careful.

8

"Don't be nervous," Parveen says as we wait outside an apartment door. I told Baba that morning that I was going to be at Nasrin's, and Parveen picked me up from school. I am getting to be a professional liar. The apartment door opens, and there stands a tall, smiling woman, probably in her fifties, wearing huge glasses and a long *chador*. She is very much a black tent with a beaming face.

"You've made it! Is this the young man you were telling me about?" the tent asks, and I look around a moment before I realize she means me.

"Yes, Goli *khanum*. This is my friend Sahar," Parveen says as she makes her way inside, tugging me by my coat. The apartment is small but well decorated. Three boys sit on a couch. They look like teenagers. Sitting in a chair is a young woman who looks to be in her mid-twenties and wears garish makeup. On the opposite side of the room is another woman sitting alone. She is demure and folded in on herself like a pile of rumpled clothes.

Goli *khanum* puts one meaty arm around me. "*Bacheha*, children, this is Sahar," she says. "She's Parveen's friend. Don't be afraid to speak in front of her. She has the same illness we do." *Illness?* I know I haven't read about all the diseases a person can have, but I never came across gender change as one of them. Parveen and I sit next to each other on a small sofa, our hips touching. I sit very straight so as not to take up too much space. Parveen takes my hand in hers, and I relax a little. The boys on the couch nod in my direction. One of them is very handsome and looks confident. He speaks first.

"I'm Jamshid. It's nice to meet you, Sahar." He smiles just like Parveen does. They both seem at ease with themselves, unlike the young woman in the corner, who continues to fiddle with her hair. "These are my two rude friends, Shahab and Behrooz," Jamshid jokes, and the shy boys nod mutely. Shahab looks very young. Behrooz looks like a girl trying to dress like a boy. Will I look that way?

"Jamshid is the perfect gentleman," Goli *khanoum* brags.

101

The young woman with the ton of makeup caked on her face speaks next. "I'm Katayoun. Welcome to our little club." I don't know if I'm ready to be a card-carrying member yet.

"Why are you here?" says the shy, fidgety woman in the corner without introducing herself.

"Don't be rude, Maryam," Parveen admonishes.

"She needs to know this isn't a game! It isn't something you just try on." Maryam's voice shakes. She looks like she hasn't slept in weeks.

"Maryam is having a hard time with her transition," Goli gently explains. It's obvious from the tension in the room that these meetings are not entirely social in nature. We sit in awkward silence as Goli *khanum* goes to the kitchen to make tea.

"Are you okay?" Parveen whispers to me.

I don't know how to answer her. Jamshid looks so confident and free. He sits relaxed, with his legs spread out as he likes. He's definitely a man. If I am to go through with this, I want to be like him. Goli returns with a tray of tea, and everyone but Maryam graciously accepts a glass.

"Does anyone have anything they want to discuss this week?" Parveen asks the group. She is obviously the team captain, while Goli is the surrogate mother.

"I was turned down from another job. I am running out of ideas about where I can work," Katayoun says.

"I am sure we can find something for you. Don't give up," Parveen says. Maryam grunts loudly in the corner.

"What is it now, Maryam?" Parveen asks.

Maryam straightens up in her chair and looks directly at Parveen. "What job is Katayoun going to get? You think they don't discriminate against her? She can't pass like you can. She doesn't have a supportive family like you do. Don't feed her any lies, Parveen."

"And what do you do?" Parveen cuts back. "Feed her despair?" It's the first time I have seen Parveen lose her composure. She's made her life sound so wonderful. Katayoun looks sadly into her teacup. I wonder what her life was like before she became a woman.

The meeting continues, and the group members talk about problems they have had facing discrimination from certain family members or places they used to frequent. Behrooz's parents have disowned him, and he is now living with Jamshid in a small apartment. Shahab went to ask a woman's family for her hand in marriage, and the family shoved him out of the house before he could even speak. Maryam does not say anything throughout the rest of the meeting. She does not look anyone in the eye, that is except for me. Her gaze makes me uneasy, and I have to keep reminding myself why I came here. As the members of the group speak, Goli *khanum* tries to ease their worries, tells them everything will get better and that Allah loves them. It's a small comfort, but it seems to keep the dissatisfied in the group hanging on. She also has her success stories, Jamshid and Parveen, as cheerleaders.

The two of them talk about how they both knew who they were from a young age. Parveen talks about dressing up and wishing she were a mermaid, so no one could see her ugly and unnatural genitalia. It's clear that Parveen's parents support her, and she continues to live with them. That seems like a rare gift in this group. Jamshid also keeps in touch with his family and manages to do well in university, though he admits that he does not tell many people that he is transsexual, especially at school.

Parveen and Jamshid also talk about how wonderful Goli *khanum* was to them when they first went to a religious meeting about transitioning that included a lecture by a mullah from Qom. The mullah said that their illness was nothing to be ashamed of and explained that turning flour into bread was not a sin—and neither was changing from a man to a woman. "According to the Islamic Republic of Iran, there is nothing in the Koran that says it is immoral to change one's gender," Jamshid says proudly. I get the feeling that no one at that meeting asked anything about homosexuality.

"Are you sure you feel that you are in the wrong body?" Jamshid asks me. I've never wanted to be a boy; it never even occurred to me before I met Parveen. From the way everyone has described the experience, I know it isn't just something you try on. There's a painful surgery, the psychological struggle to get used to your new body, and the prospect of having no family left to support you. All that seems to be only the beginning.

"After my transition, my family felt that their son had died," Goli says. "They even wore mourning clothes for forty days."

Do I feel like I was born in the wrong body? I know how I feel when Nasrin walks in a room. I feel strong and weak. I feel proud and ashamed. I feel love for her and hate for myself. I want to be clean of my feelings for her because they are wrong. Everyone knows that.

"Yes," I say. "I feel like I'm in the wrong body."

"You're lying," Maryam says from her corner. Everyone yells at her for being insensitive. They trust me completely. Goli tells Maryam to serve everyone more tea, and Maryam reluctantly complies, shuffling in her slippers across the floor to the kitchen.

"It's a big thing you're doing," Jamshid says. "Admitting your illness. It takes courage, and we're so proud of you."

I feel their acceptance, and it feels good. It's nice to belong somewhere. It feels good to have this kind of support from a group that understands what it means to be different. It's unusual in our culture, but it exists. Nasrin and I might have a chance.

9

THIS IS THE LAST thing I want to do. The last place I want to be. I have to be here because it would look suspicious otherwise, but I wish I could have taken some of those drugs that Ali has around beforehand.

I hate shopping for myself. It's tiring, I can never afford anything I would actually want, and the clothes I prefer are not entirely fashionable or ladylike. Shopping with Nasrin is both agony and pleasure. I love seeing her in glamorous clothes. I love the high she gets from a new pair of shoes or a dress. I love that we can be in a store full of only women and she can twirl in front of a mirror freely while other women stare at her in envy of their younger years. I love that she always asks for my opinion.

At the moment Nasrin is trying on wedding dresses. "What

do we think of this one?" the genial shopgirl asks. She's skinny, in tight black jeans, black high heels, and a white silk blouse. Mrs. Mehdi and Nasrin look at the latest wedding dress on display and begin arguing. This dress is traditional, white with lace sleeves and a lace bodice with a long train in the back. I sit in the corner, watching the two of them bicker while other clerks and customers mill about with their own wedding dress dilemmas and triumphs. The hell I will go to because of my girl-loving heart will look a great deal like this store.

When we arrived at the dress shop, we had to use an intercom to be buzzed in. The store has no windows, so all the women are allowed to remove their head scarves if they so choose, which is all of us in the store. For once, though, I wish I'd continued wearing my manteau and head scarf, because I feel underdressed.

All the other women wear so much makeup. Some have shaved their eyebrows and tattooed on thicker, more luxurious ones, while others have dunked their lashes in so much mascara, I can't imagine how they will ever be able to wash it off.

Mrs. Mehdi is again telling Nasrin why this dress is "perfect," and Nasrin of course has her eye on another one. They have been arguing over every dress, and I am not brave enough to try to play referee. Mrs. Mehdi looks like she is ready to strangle her daughter, and Nasrin is practically frothing at the mouth.

I haven't told Nasrin about my plans yet. It's not that I want to catch her off guard, I just don't need to put more pressure on her yet, and I don't want her to talk me out of the only thing I can think of to keep us together. It doesn't sound so bad. Parveen and Jamshid have full lives, and Jamshid has more rights as a man than I do as a woman. He can wear short sleeves; he can have two wives or more if he can provide for them. I can't even get one. It seems ideal, if I don't think about Maryam and her distorted and furious face.

Nasrin rolls her eyes at her mother and turns to give me a pout. She knows how much I hate this. She texted me late last night about how sorry she was to make me go through dress fittings. I didn't text back. I don't think she's having much fun, either.

"Try it on, Nasrin. What can it hurt?" Mrs. Mehdi says with irritation. The attendant picks up the dress, leading Nasrin to the changing rooms in back. This leaves Mrs. Mehdi and me alone. Most of the time we get along fine. She tells me stories about my mother and the baby chicks they used to play with when they were little kids. Lately, though, she's been quieter, and I find it unnerving. Everything is very polite between us. No frosty overtones or snide remarks, but she's steely eyed now. I am not sure when that changed. Sometimes I wonder if she knows . . . No. Nasrin and I are always careful.

As if to chase away these thoughts, Mrs. Mehdi sits next to me and pats my leg in good spirits. "I'm exhausted," she says. "Nasrin is just as stubborn as her father."

"She will decide on a dress eventually," I say. "She's pretty good about making decisions." Good at making the right decisions about the right kind of person who can give her the right kind of life. This marriage is her playing it safe. The only time she's decided to do that. Mrs. Mehdi drinks from the tea a clerk freshened up for her a few moments ago. The staff fawn over Nasrin and her mother, and I know both of the Mehdi women love it. I wonder if my mother, growing up with all her wealth, relished the attention while it came to her. I try not to think about that.

"My own wedding seems like ages ago," Mrs. Mehdi says. Nasrin and I used to love to look at all the photographs of her parents' special day, with my parents in the background as special guests. My mother was gorgeous. Nasrin even admitted that she was making the bride look bad in comparison. That always made me very proud. "Your mother was such a good friend," Mrs. Mehdi recalls. "I was so nervous."

A few feet away a girl emerges from the dressing room, squealing in delight over the dress she has put on. Seeing her daughter, the mother starts crying. My mother and I wouldn't make such a scene. She would probably realize that I wouldn't feel comfortable in an elaborate, frilly wedding dress and suggest a plain white dress instead. We would get ice cream afterward and talk about my classes. We might have.

"I needed my best friend there that day," Mrs. Mehdi says sadly. "It's important, deciding to spend your life with someone even if you think he isn't the perfect choice." This surprises me a little. True, I don't see Mr. and Mrs. Mehdi look at each other the way Maman and Baba did, but my parents were rare. Nasrin would sometimes sleep over at my house when she was younger, usually because her parents had gotten into some big fight. These fights were occasional but lasted a few days. Mrs. Mehdi would criticize something small about her husband, like the way he chewed at dinner or that he smelled of body odor, and Mr. Mehdi would yell and scream. Neither would talk to the other for a few days, but they got over it.

Nasrin was now unfazed by their quarrels, but when we were eight years old, she would cry in my arms and I'd smooth her hair. Sometimes my *maman* would come in the room and cheer us up.

"I am glad you are going to be at the wedding for Nasrin. She will need you," Mrs. Mehdi says.

"She will be fine," I say. "It should be a lot of fun." Really, I want to knock over all of the stupid mannequins with ridiculous neon-colored wigs on their heads.

Mrs. Mehdi takes another sip of tea and eyes me coolly. "It won't be long before it's your special day, I'm sure."

I bring out one of my many rehearsed lines. "Oh, I'm not ready for anything like that yet. I still have so much work ahead of me."

"Well, someday you may want to start a family of your own, just like Nasrin does. I can't wait to be a grandmother! Though I don't look old enough to be a grandmother, do I?" Nasrin does not get her vanity from her father.

"You look very young. I'm sure Nasrin will wait until you grow older to give you grandchildren." I don't know if she really possesses maternal instincts. I never imagined her as a mother, and we've never talked about having children. Is that why she is doing this?

"Nasrin loves kids," Mrs. Mehdi says. "You've seen the way she looks after the younger children at parties." She's right, but that's because Nasrin is a kid herself. I never thought her fondness for children came from a deep desire to have her own, but maybe I didn't want to see it.

"Yes. Yes she's good with children."

"If they have Reza's eyes and Nasrin's smile, I think we will have some little heartbreakers on our hands, won't we?" Another happy family. Not like mine. The store clerk comes back into the room, leading Nasrin, who looks gorgeous in the white dress her mother insisted she try on. I sit on my hands.

"Oh, Nasrin, you look beautiful!" Mrs. Mehdi exclaims. "This is the one! This is the one for you!" She's already picked out Nasrin's life, why not the dress? Nasrin admires herself in the mirror and inspects the same problem areas she has had through all of high school. First she looks at her chest and wishes it were a little bigger. Then she looks at her backside and wishes it were a little smaller.

"What do you think, Sahar?"

"I think you look perfect." I think this whole thing has gotten out of hand and I want to take you away from it. "Do *you* like it?" Nasrin looks at me with so much affection, I think I might burst. People don't often ask Nasrin her opinion.

"I like the other one better," she admits, and before her mother can protest I butt in.

"Then go try it on. You will look beautiful in that one, too."

Nasrin smiles at me and steps down from the little makeshift stage with mirrors surrounding her. The attendant follows her with the dress Nasrin selected, leaving me with Mrs. Mehdi again.

"I thought it was a lovely dress," Mrs. Mehdi grumbles.

"It was. But it's her special day." Mrs. Mehdi raises an eyebrow. It's the look she used to give my mother when they would disagree. Maman always took it in stride. Funny how daughters mimic their mothers.

"Sometimes the best things for us aren't necessarily the things we want," she says, and it's such a loaded statement I'm not sure how to answer. If she does know about me, the way I am, I wish she'd let me know. Just tell me what to do—and I don't mean just marry some man and have babies. But she has nothing to say at the moment. I continue to sit on my hands and wait for Nasrin to come out. When she reappears, she looks even more stunning than the last time. I can't help but stand and approach her when she steps up on the platform. Other women in the shop stop to compliment Mrs. Mehdi on her beautiful daughter.

Nasrin meets my gaze and smiles softly. "How do I look?" Don't cry. Don't cry. Nasrin and I haven't discussed what happens to us once she is married. I can't just come over all the time and kiss her in her bedroom. Homosexuality is dangerous, but adulterers can be stoned to death. We can't continue if she goes through with marrying him. Both of us are afraid to bring it up. I can't think this way; everyone will notice. I do my best to shake off my gloom.

"I like the other dress better, but you look beautiful," Mrs. Mehdi says.

"I think this is the one!" Nasrin exclaims, and the store attendant looks so happy, she may cry. The rest of the women who have stopped to watch give a bloodcurdling shriek in unison to commemorate the joyous occasion.

"You made the right decision," I say sadly. Nasrin looks at her mother and her mother shrugs. I sit next to Mrs. Mehdi while the women of the store crowd around Nasrin.

"I guess we can't always get what we want," Mrs. Mehdi whispers to me. She is talking about the dress. But now I know she knows about me. I can't tell which of us is the bigger coward. I sit on my hands again, watching Nasrin twirl in front of the mirror. I wish she would be so confident in all her decisions.

10

MY GRADES HAVE BEEN slipping a little. We have three tests a day. It's been that way since middle school, and I've always been near the top of my class, but lately the only math I can do is counting the days until Sahar's wedding, and the only questions I can concentrate on are the ones I have about surgery. Time is running out if I want to go through with my transformation. I want to end up like Jamshid. He knows who he is, he goes to school, and he goes about his life as an actual man. But Shahab and Behrooz look like sad little boys who got in way over their head. What if I end up like them?

Baba isn't home yet, and I should be studying physics, but my mind won't settle on the pages in front of me. This evening it's whirling with possibilities of what I will look like after I change. I don't think I'll ever be a muscleman or anything, and I'll probably have a baby face. At least I won't have to bleach my mustache anymore. I get up and go into Baba's bedroom. The room is tidy because Baba is hardly ever in here. He usually sleeps on the sofa or in a kitchen chair, and then only when weariness overtakes him.

Maman's side of the room is completely intact. Her perfume bottles, designer brands from Europe, are still on the dresser. Expensive perfume was one of the few luxuries she allowed herself. All the photos of the three of us on her bedside table are collecting dust.

I go to Baba's closet and open the heavy door, revealing a wardrobe fit for a mortuary. The black suit coat will do. That and a button-up shirt, though it's a shame Baba isn't my size. I strip to my underwear, looking in the full-length mirror to the right of the bed. Nasrin is the one who inspects herself, pinching her hips and looking at everything that could be wrong. Now I am the one. My chest is too big and my hips are wide. Can that be fixed? Jamshid is flat chested, but he also has small hips. It's like he was meant to be a boy. The mirror seems pretty convinced that I was meant to be a girl.

Maybe if I just flatten my breasts a little. Flatten them a lot. I put on one of Baba's white button-up shirts, and it's so big that I look swallowed up. I roll up the sleeves at the cuff. Next are his slacks, black and too long for me, but I put them on. Tucking in my shirt, I imagine Nasrin in the background, getting out of the shower and complaining about how she has nothing to wear for a party we have to go to. Women are insufferable. I can think that as a man.

She will tell me to wear the black sport coat and say she's glad I don't have too much facial hair. It's a fantasy, but I relish it as I pull my hair back and put it under a fedora I know my *baba* hasn't worn since his school days. I look at myself again. It doesn't work. I'm a girl. I close my eyes, wishing I could transform into a tall, handsome man with strong wrists and shoulders. There's Nasrin behind me in a dress, picking lint off my shoulders and telling me that we are going to be late for whatever stupid social occasion her mother has roped us into. I open my eyes.

"Sahar?" I freeze as I see Baba's reflection in the mirror. He's home early from the workshop! How didn't I hear him come in? Damn him for being so quiet!

"It's for one of Nasrin's music videos! They need a boy for the dance routine!" I have become such a fast liar. If I don't cry, he might actually believe me.

"Oh," Baba says, looking at me. Even if he doesn't believe my lie, he wouldn't believe the actual reason I am in his clothes. I have never been afraid of Baba. I know some girls in my class have deeply religious fathers with strict rules. Other girls have fathers who discipline them physically. Baba is so gentle that it has turned pathetic these past few years. I think about how Goli *khanum*'s family mourned their loss of a son. I don't know if I could put Baba through that. Though he's so deep in his grief, I doubt he would notice I was gone.

"It doesn't suit you," he says.

I take off the hat and look at my reflection again. "No. I suppose not. But it's important . . . for the video project." I want to get out of these clothes. I don't know what he is trying to accomplish by just standing there.

"Nasrin is always getting you to do these crazy things." He chuckles, but the sound makes my eyes well up. I can't let him see me cry.

"I'm going to change . . ." I whisper, and he nods, turning his back and walking into the kitchen. Tears fall from my eyes, and I try not to make too many gurgling noises. My nose runs as I look at how big this shirt actually is on me.

"I can make dinner tonight, Sahar. What would you like

to eat?" Baba hasn't cooked a meal in five years. The shock is enough to stop my tears.

"Um, *aab gosht* would be fine if you have lamb?" I know we have lamb. I do all the grocery shopping.

"That sounds fine. You like *aab gosht*!" he calls. I don't actually. But it's simple to make. Whenever Baba offered to cook, Maman and I would ask him to make it. Everyone in my family always spares one another's feelings. It leaves little room for honesty. I put my jeans back on and hang the too long trousers back in Baba's closet along with his shirt. They look better on the hangers than they do on me. How do Jamshid and Parveen look so natural, so confident? Maybe if—*when*—I go through the surgery, I will look the part too. Maybe.

"Mrs. Mehdi called me. She says there is a party for the bride and groom this Friday." Baba keeps opening and shutting the cabinet doors as he calls to me, and I can tell he's struggling to find the ingredients.

"Don't those two have enough parties?" I call back. Nasrin told me about this one during one of our last "study sessions." Our head scarves came in handy to hide the bite marks on our necks. Nasrin has been putting lots of makeup on her neck to cover her bruises. I relish them. She's mine and I don't want her to forget it. But we need to stop. If Reza were to catch us, if anyone were to catch us, we would be done for. The love bite on my neck could one day be replaced by rope burn.

I pull a T-shirt over my head and notice the way my hips and breasts are showcased. I'm such a girl.

I walk into the kitchen, where Baba is stirring chickpeas and potatoes. He's facing the stove, with his back to me. "If you want to buy a dress you can. I've been commissioned for a piece, and you never treat yourself." Dress shopping. He doesn't know me at all. I wipe my eyes and nose, and fan my face to give myself air. I don't want him to ask more questions. I slump in a chair by the kitchen table, don't comment when I see he hasn't added salt.

Baba turns to me, still stirring. "There you are," he says. "My clothes don't even look good on me, never mind on a beautiful girl like you,"

Why is it now that he is choosing to be a parent? "I'm not beautiful."

"You aren't?"

"Baba, please don't humor me. I've had a long . . . month." More like a long few years.

Baba stops stirring the pot and turns to look at me again. My face feels hot. Baba has never made me angry before. Maman and I always had arguments. Sometimes Baba would mollify us. Sometimes he would bow out gracefully and let us deal with our issues. Maman and I would fight about little things, like how often I could play with Nasrin. Most of our arguments were about Nasrin, now that I think about it.

"You're a beautiful girl," he says.

I've never felt that way. I don't feel comfortable in my skin, and that has nothing to do with my gender. Growing up around Nasrin made me pale in comparison. But I never cared because I felt beautiful being her friend. She chose me.

The pot boils over. Baba backs away quickly before water splashes on him. I rush to the stove and lower the heat. I look at him. He can't even boil water. He takes his manhood for granted. What I could do as a man. Who I could *be* in this country . . . I would leave him in the dust. My jaw clenches. I can change. I don't have to be stuck like this.

"It has been a while since I've cooked," he says.

"Five years. It's been five years since you've cooked." I turn off the stove and watch the boiling bubbles pop in the pot. Maman died five years ago of a heart attack. Her smoking probably didn't help. I told her to stop. She just smiled sweetly and told me not to worry so much. That's what we do. Smile and not worry so much. Riot in the street? Smile and don't worry so much. See the swinging bodies in the square? Smile and don't worry so much. Can't be with the person you love because it's against the law? Smile, damn it.

"I'm not very good in the kitchen," Baba says.

"You don't try! At anything!" He balks at my yelling. His hesitation only eggs me on. "I do everything! I do everything to remind you that we're still living, and you don't care to participate."

Baba doesn't protest. Most fathers would tell me to shut up or send me to my room. He sits and lowers his head to his hands, running his fingers through his hair. I should back off, but I've had enough. Someone needs to feel my rage.

"Maman left one child behind, not two! You're supposed to take care of me. Why won't you take care of me?"

"I don't know." It's the best and most honest answer he's ever given me. He looks lost. He looks like he's been kicked in the face. He makes it difficult to be angry with him. I look back at the bubbling pot on the stove.

"You forgot to add salt," I say, and as soon as I do he's up and finding the salt in one of the cabinets. He adds some to the pot and stirs it in, looking at me as though he's asking for permission.

"I always forget salt, don't I?" He's finally noticing his shortcomings. Normally I would tell him it doesn't matter or that the dish doesn't really need salt.

"Yes. You always used to forget. Even when you tried."

He nods and asks me to sit down while he continues to prepare the meal.

"Your Maman didn't like my cooking at all, did she?" Baba asks. The question makes me smile a little. I shake my head. He chuckles, and it's about time.

11

"WELL, AT LEAST THEY are serving decent food," Ali says as he tosses another grape into his mouth. Baba decided not to come to the party now that he is actually grieving. Ali was more than willing to be my male escort.

"You look really good," he says. "Nasrin should get engaged more often. You'd turn into a fashionista."

I'm glad Ali is here, but sometimes I wish he would just shut up. I took up Baba's offer and asked Parveen to go dress shopping with me. She was surprised at my wanting to buy a dress, but I explained it was for a party. I think all my groaning in the dress shop convinced her that I really want to be a man.

There are so many guests here, even more than last time. The Mehdis hired caterers, and Soraya is off for the evening to enjoy the festivities. She is dressed in a simple brown dress that is long enough to cover her thick, overworked legs. She wears a white head scarf, doing her best to dress up. Soraya's daughter, Sima, is here, too. She gave me advice for the university entrance examinations. Even though I tried my best to listen, I couldn't keep my eyes off Nasrin, who has had her *namzad*, her fiancé, right next to her all evening.

"It was a mistake to come tonight. No one would have noticed if I wasn't here." I'm muttering to Ali, who not so subtly glances at Cyrus Mehdi's ass. Ali has always liked boys who are dumb and cute. Cyrus is talking to Mr. Mehdi's business associates and can't stop tugging on his shirt collar. Mr. Mehdi just smacks his son's back, laughing and being the man of the hour. Mr. Mehdi always likes to be the center of attention. Nasrin gets that from him. While Cyrus tries his best to appease some old businessmen, Dariush is across the room, chatting with Sima. She laughs a little, and Dariush looks pleased. I would worry about Sima, but then Soraya comes to her daughter's side and the three of them continue to talk.

"I'm surprised you haven't been at Nasrin's beck and call all evening," Ali says.

"That's because the groom is always with her! Doesn't he have to use the bathroom?"

"He would probably bring her in there. Bathrooms are sexy sometimes." I don't want to know how he came to that conclusion. "Besides, I thought we were here to get to know the enemy."

"What do you mean?" I ask. Reza's palm is at Nasrin's lower back while they talk to some doctor types. You aren't married yet! Don't get so carried away with your hands!

"He must have a weakness. Something unappealing that might make the family rethink giving their precious daughter away. A secret drug habit, perhaps? He has two wives already? Maybe he's related to Saddam Hussein."

"Ali, be serious."

"I'm just saying that you can't compete if you don't better acquaint yourself with the competition." He has a point, and I do have some morbid curiosity. What do Reza and Nasrin even talk about? She's barely an adult and doesn't know anything about medicine, and he certainly doesn't know anything about her. Another part of me doesn't want to know him. I feel guilty enough as it is, spending time alone with Nasrin.

"He's busy talking with all the grown-ups. Doesn't he feel ashamed having a wife half his age?" I ask.

"He's a man. He can do whatever he wants," Ali says flippantly, and pops another grape into his mouth. He picks them off the stems from bunches on the table rather than just taking a small bunch on to a plate. I hate when people do that. "He is a handsome man. And he didn't even have to get a nose job or anything." Many young people in Tehran get nose jobs. It isn't uncommon to see men and women alike walking around with bandages on their noses without embarrassment. Three girls in my class had nose jobs at the same time. After the bandages came off, I couldn't tell them apart from one another for a week.

"Nasrin hasn't even looked at me all night," I grumble.

Ali laughs. "That doesn't mean she hasn't seen you. Don't you notice how red her face gets when she knows you're nearby? I'm telling you, Parveen knows her fashion." I blush, realizing my twin sisters are more exposed than usual tonight. "You and Parveen have been spending a lot of time together," Ali adds.

"She's a nice girl," I say.

"You know you aren't her type," he says.

I laugh, glad the music is so loud. "Why does everything have to be about lust and sex with you?"

"Because everything else is boring, Sahar! So if you don't

129

have a thing for her, why do you spend so much time with her?" I'm not going to tell him what I'm planning. He would probably just laugh at me and tell me how foolish an idea it is. I don't care if the plan is naive; it's all I have right now.

"Parveen's kept me distracted, and she's a good listener."

"Whatever you say, cousin." Ali takes great strides across the crowded room and stops in the middle, looking over one shoulder to me. He raises his eyebrows, and I don't want to do this, but I would rather chaperone Ali than let him loose around Nasrin at her own party. I trail him as he approaches the doctors and Nasrin. He was right. She's blushing.

"Nasrin! My, you two make a handsome couple!" Ali exclaims as he pats Reza on the back. I make my way into the circle and look at Nasrin. She stares at Ali, but her face becomes an even deeper shade of red.

Nasrin makes the introduction. "Reza, this is Sahar's cousin, Ali. Don't listen to half the stories he will tell you."

"*Baleh, salam.* It's very nice to meet you." The two men shake hands, and I notice one of the other doctors in the group looks nervous. Ali notices, too. When he lets go of Reza's hand, he addresses the doctor.

"Hello, Nasser. Haven't seen you in ages!" The young

doctor blushes and politely nods. I'd rather not think about how they know each other. Nasser mentions something about getting some water and leaves the group. The other physicians continue to chatter about doctor things, and I hope I never sound as elitist as they do. Nasrin finally glances at me. She looks miserable. She has a smile and too much makeup plastered on her face. Her unhappiness is in her eyes. There are tomes of stories resting there if anyone cared to see them.

"It's nice to see you again, Sahar," Doctor Superman says to me, and I try not to cringe. It feels like there is a mouse jumping on a trampoline inside my stomach.

"Congratulations," I say, taking my eyes off Nasrin, and reminding myself to stop staring at her.

"Sahar, I know this is a difficult time for you," Reza says, and I panic. I look at Ali, who wears a *This-should-be-interesting* face. Does Reza know . . . Did Nasrin tell him? I glance over at Nasrin, but she still has a saccharine smile on her face.

"What do you mean, sir?" I add the *sir* not out of respect but because he is so much older than I am.

"I know Nasrin is like a sister to you. You two have done everything together, and I am taking her away from you. But

I want you to know that we aren't moving far, and you are always welcome in our home. If anything, I hope you and I can be friends, too." He actually looks sympathetic and sincere.

"I, um . . . I appreciate that. I'm going to miss her. So very much." I make direct eye contact with Nasrin. She looks away. She can't keep up the charade otherwise. Reza and Nasrin don't touch each other, but they stand close, and they look like they fit together. Even when I change, I will never be as tall as Reza.

"So you're a doctor?" Ali asks Reza, drawing me out of my own head for a moment.

"I'm just an intern. I'm just starting, but I enjoy it, helping patients. It's very rewarding."

"What a coincidence! Did you know that all Sahar dreams about is being a surgeon?" I could kill Ali. Reza looks at me with great enthusiasm, and again he seems so sincere. It makes me feel wretched.

"That's wonderful! Have you decided what kind of surgery interests you?" I shake my head. The more I talk with him the worse I feel. How can Nasrin be with him but think of me? I shudder to think about the rest of their life together.

"You two have so much in common," Ali says. My eyes bug

out of my face, but Nasrin coughs and I relax my expression. I want to wipe that roguish grin off Ali's face. Particularly when Ali looks in Nasrin's direction. "You two must be so excited for the big day!" Nasrin's nostrils flare despite the exaggerated smile she still manages to wear. I don't think she realizes how long she will have to play the part of adoring wife. "How did you two meet, anyway?"

Ali is unbelievable. People never ask these questions, because it's no one's business. We all know he came to the Mehdis' house and asked for their daughter's hand in marriage. He probably figured he needed someone to cook and clean for him, maybe pop out some heirs. This is usually how these things go. It's an arrangement.

"Well, Dariush and I are friends. When I came over to visit, Nasrin would be home sometimes. She always managed to put a smile on my face, but at first I didn't think anything of it." I want to slam my head against a wall. He actually has feelings for her? This wasn't supposed to happen! He was supposed to be a creepy older man who couldn't find anyone his own age. He was supposed to be a wolf in sheep's clothing. "But then as I went about my rounds, all I could think about was something funny Nasrin had said or how well she imitated her brother. I hadn't laughed so much in a very long time. I knew I had to have her as my wife. I came back to visit with Nasrin and her family over a period of a few weeks, and eventually they graciously accepted my proposal. I don't think I've ever been happier." Reza looks at Nasrin the same way I do.

"That's a lovely story," I say, and Nasrin stares at me in fear. She thinks I'm going to expose her. Expose *us*. I should. Reza just beams at me, and I want to smash his teeth in with a crowbar.

"Will you excuse me?" Nasrin asks. "I have to use the ladies' room." She bolts for the back of the house. Reza looks shocked, and Ali just grins. He notices Nasser from earlier and excuses himself. This leaves Reza and me alone in a room full of people.

"Is she all right?" Reza asks me. His eyes are full of worry and regret, as though he may have said something wrong.

"No, she gets easily embarrassed sometimes. You wouldn't think it, because she loves attention so much." He takes a deep breath, and I can't decide whether to wish he were dead or to sympathize. It's not easy being in love with Nasrin.

"We're still learning things about one another. I'm actually jealous of you. You know practically everything about her."

Yes, Reza, I do know everything about her. I know she cries when she sees stray dogs, while most other Iranians couldn't care less. All we have in Iran is stray dogs. Hardly anyone has a dog as a pet. If it were up to Nasrin, she would adopt all of them and have them ruin the Mehdis' house. I know Nasrin hates cooking, and all she can make is eggs, though she hates the smell. I know Nasrin moans when I bite at her earlobe. She almost always whispers my name afterward.

"Sometimes I feel like she is keeping something from me," Reza continues. "I know, it's foolish to expect to know some- one so quickly, but I want her to trust me." I don't know where this sensitive male thing is coming from, but it's making me steadily more uncomfortable.

"You actually love her, don't you?" It surprises me that I ask it. He grins and I don't do the same back. If anything, his love just makes me angry.

"She's the one for me." No. She's mine. She's been mine and always will be, you son of a bitch. My face feels hot, and I hope I haven't broken out in a sweat. "Are you all right, Sahar? You look flushed." Oh, you want to be the doctor now?

"It's just so hot in here." Before I know it, he's gone and grabbed a chair for me. While I'm seated, trying to calm down, he has come back from the kitchen with a cool washcloth. He offers it to me, and I want to swat it out of his hand and then bite him like a crazed lioness. Instead I accept his gesture and pat my forehead with the offending cloth. "Thank you."

"*Khahesh mikonam*—you're welcome. Would you like some water?" I shake my head and try to give him some friendly facial gesture. All I manage is a grimace. Now he's just standing in front of me, looking worried. Like I'm some silly girl to be pitied. I shouldn't be angry with him. He isn't the problem. I am.

"Is everything all right?" Mrs. Mehdi asks us as she walks over to me. She instinctively rubs my back in circles like my *maman* did.

"I'm fine. Reza was kind enough to look after me," I say politely.

"Do you need some water?" Mrs. Mehdi asks.

"No. I'm fine, thank you." Keep it together. Steady your breathing. Smile.

"He's a sweet man, isn't he? Definitely good enough for our Nasrin," Mrs. Mehdi says, and Reza blushes like he's a damn woman. I breathe steadily to cool down. "Where is

Nasrin?" Mrs. Mehdi asks, searching the expansive room for her prized jewel.

"She ran off to the bathroom. She seems a bit . . . Well it's been a lot of parties lately. She might be overwhelmed," Prince Charming says.

"I was just in the bathroom. I didn't see her anywhere near there," Mrs. Mehdi says, looking at me.

"I'll find her," I volunteer, and I stand and then walk through the crowd. Ali is chatting up Cyrus Mehdi, and the poor fool doesn't realize that Ali is hitting on him in the suave, masculine way he has learned over the years. Dariush Mehdi and Sima are talking, close to each other but far enough apart that they won't create a scandal. Dariush ducks his head in embarrassment while Sima laughs over some joke I am sure they are sharing. I don't know if Mrs. Mehdi would approve of either of her sons' company for the evening.

I exit through the kitchen and into the backyard. Nasrin sits by the swimming pool, her face illuminated like she is some divine creature from the ocean. There is a giant fence surrounding the yard, so no prying eyes can see Nasrin tan in her bikini during the summer. I take off my high heels and sit down next to her, dipping my feet into the pool.

"I don't know how you wear high heels so often. My feet are in agony." It isn't a funny statement, but it's all I can do to make her feel a little better. "He's . . . well, he's nice. He loves you, too, which is interesting." I don't know why I am comforting her. Someone should be comforting me.

"He's very nice. I am a lucky woman."

"You don't sound lucky."

"There's nothing wrong with him. He's a little boring, but he's handsome. He has a good job, he helps people, and he even gets along with my mother. He listens to her stories like they are fascinating."

"Your mother should divorce your father and marry your fiancé instead." If only. Nasrin finally looks at me and puts her hand over mine. It's never felt so heavy before.

"He's a wonderful man. But I don't feel anything for him the way I do for you. And that terrifies me." I gulp at her admission. I will replay her saying it over and over in my head tonight.

"Don't marry him." I whisper it, just in case anyone finds us in the darkness.

"And what would you have me do? Marry you?"

"Yes."

She squeezes my hand.

"Stop living in a fantasy. You might make me start believing, and I can't afford to do that." I don't say anything else after that. But I do believe we could work. Does this make me delusional? We sit together for a few moments. Then she stands up and walks back inside. I don't follow her.

12

"I CAUGHT THE YOUNG man at the grocery store looking at me. It was discreet, but I could tell he liked me. And it felt so good, for him to look at me that way. Like he really wanted me. Like he knew I was a woman." Katayoun is telling her story. She looks so hopeful, but I can't stop looking at the clock. Time is running out. I'm politely waiting for Katayoun to finish. I don't need emotional support—I need to figure out how to do this. How it's going to work. How I'm going to change.

"Is it wrong for me to feel like . . . I mean, I'm not a loose person," Katayoun continues, and I feel selfish for wanting her to stop, but I need to get on with it already.

"No, *azizam,* it's not wrong. A woman likes to feel beautiful every so often." Goli *khanum* is kind with her surrogate children. They listen to her advice because she was one of the first, a pioneer. She's lived longer as her true self than they have. She's lived longer as her true self than I ever will, if I ever make this change. After hearing their stories at the last meeting, I know none of their struggles have been easy. Jamshid even talks about how hard it was between him and his sister once he transitioned. His sister felt like she had lost her best friend and gained a stranger as a brother. He says she's getting better about calling him Jamshid instead of Niloufar.

Katayoun has unshed tears in her eyes, too embarrassed to let them spill. "I'm just tired of feeling sorry for myself. I sit in my room all day and wonder if it would have been better if I just died."

"Probably."

Everyone hisses and gasps at Maryam's retort. It's the only thing she's said all meeting. Maryam is angry. I envy her sometimes. How easy it is for her anger to proudly be on display. I always feel guilty when I get angry. Baba has been working on a custom-made dining room set, but I can tell his heart isn't in it. I shouldn't scold him, but I do. Well, I won't be around much longer, anyway. I doubt he will accept me once I change. I can stay with Ali. Meanwhile, I feel the wedding getting closer. I have a recurring dream about Reza and his stupid smile. He's holding Nasrin's hand as she stands next to him, grinning beneath fearful eyes. Nasrin keeps calling out for me, but I never come. When I get there, they vanish right before my eyes. I always wake up after that.

"I just don't know why Allah would do this. Why would the Merciful One create me one way when I'm supposed to be another way? Why do I always feel like I switched one prison for another? My body for my country." Katayoun is sobbing. Parveen puts an arm around her shoulder. Emotions take up too much time. We need to hurry.

"But isn't it wonderful that you live in Iran?" Parveen consoles her. "Where the government recognizes your struggle? Do you know that there are places in the West that the government would never help pay for the gift of an operation?" Goli *khanum* told us in the last meeting that Iran has the second-highest number of sexual reassignment surgeries, after Thailand.

"Oh yes," Maryam says. "So wonderful to be given the ultimatum of changing your gender or dying as a sinner." She usually offers her disdain for Goli *khanum* and her platitudes by way of a loud harrumph or an exaggerated eye roll. Tonight she is more verbal than usual, and part of me wants to tell her to shut up so I can have my turn to speak. They must let me speak.

"It was just nice feeling like I could pass," Katayoun says. "You always ruin everything, Maryam." Maryam has no rebuttal.

"Don't worry, Katayoun. Maryam is just jealous because you are much prettier than she is." Jamshid is always kind, but I've noticed that he's especially kind to Katayoun. They would make a nice pair. They fit. Man and Woman. Woman and Man.

Katayoun smiles as she wipes her eyes with her fingers. "I'm sorry. It's probably just all the hormones I've been taking," Katayoun murmurs. *Hormones.* I need those.

Everyone has a story, but as I hear more I find it hard to relate. I lied when I said I was born in the wrong body. I don't always like my body or that I have love handles. I don't always like that as a woman I have fewer options than men, even men that aren't as smart as I am.

But I never feel like my body is a trap.

If anything, I feel like my love is a trap.

I don't mind having to change, if that's what it takes to be with Nasrin, but I *do* mind watching her live a lie.

"Where can I get hormones?" I ask, and the eyes in the room turn to me. I suppose it was an insensitive time to ask. They don't understand. I need this now.

"Well, you'd have to visit a doctor for those," Behrooz says. His suit this week fits him a little better than the sweater he wore last time. It makes him look less lumpy.

"Not necessarily," Shahab interjects. "You could get some from a dealer." That sounds good. I bet Ali could get me some. I could subtly ask, though I'm not sure how one subtly asks for hormones.

"Yes, but illegal hormones can be dangerous," Goli *khanoum* says. "You can never be sure what's actually in them. You remember poor Shahnaz and how sick she got." Shahnaz is one of Goli *khanoum*'s past children.

"It's just, I was wondering how long it would take to have the operation. I'm ready, and how long do the surgery and recovery take?" Maryam raises an eyebrow at me in amusement, and Jamshid looks at me in the most condescending way.

Parveen takes her arm away from Katayon's shoulders and places her hand on mine. Her soft, and very large, hand. "*Joonam*, it isn't so simple as just popping into a doctor's office," she says gently.

"What do you mean?" They were supposed to be happy about this. They were supposed to let me be a part of their group. Goli *khanum* looks at me with mirth in her eyes, but I also see understanding there.

"You have to visit a surgeon," Jamshid explains. "Before they can even begin to operate, you need to have psych evaluations. It can take up to six months before they deem you as transsexual." I feel like I am being choked.

"But I need this soon. I need this now!" I stand up from the plush sofa, and the room suffocates me. "I can't wait that long. It will be too late." I need to tell Nasrin before the wedding when my surgery date will be. Then she'll call it off. She will wait for me. She *must* wait for me.

"Too late for what?" Parveen asks. I need to be careful. Don't say too much. Don't say anything about *her*.

"It's just . . . It's difficult not knowing where I belong."

Jamshid takes a sip from his teacup, and even the way he does it is so masculine, holding it from underneath. How does he know how to do that?

"Well, after a few visits with a psychiatrist they will know that about you," Goli *khanum* says. "Then you will have to prepare. Register your status with the government,

145

take hormones, and the surgery is not easy. It's painful, and the recovery period keeps you in bed for quite some time." I should have thought of this earlier. Of course you cannot walk around Tehran as though you just had a nose job. Maybe if I had spent less time on school I would have thought of this plan sooner. I would have met Parveen earlier, and the seed would have been planted.

"Plus, you aren't quite yet an adult," Parveen says. "You would have to have your father's permission." It's the last nail in the coffin. I was naive. I wasn't thinking. Everything has gone wrong.

"What's your rush?" Maryam asks. She now sits at the edge of her chair in the far corner of the living room. Her eyes are fierce with passion, and it's the most engaged I've ever seen her in a meeting.

"I'm just ready. That's all. It's important that I change as soon as possible." The young men on the couch in front of me nod in understanding. They know what it's like to be trapped. Maryam, however, is unrelenting. She eyes me, donning a vicious smirk that recognizes something in me. She's figured me out.

"It's a change. Of that you can be certain. One you would

never want to take lightly. Especially if you had a choice."
Maryam's arms are folded. She's so smug.

"I don't have a choice. This is all I have. I need this, whether
you will help me or not." I address the group as though I'm
going to war. I am, in a way. With my body, my feelings, my
circumstances—these are things I want to fight for.

Parveen looks up at me, her sad expression letting me
know that my dreams won't come true. "There is no fairy
godmother, Cinderella. Life doesn't work that way. If you're
patient and go through the steps, you will be able to change.
But there's a lot of energy that goes into a transformation,"
Parveen says. I slump back onto the sofa. Everyone is staring
at me. I can feel it, and my face grows hot.

"I can get you hormones," Katayoun says in a quiet voice.

"Yes. Please."

Parveen rubs my back, and I'm so tired. So very tired.

"Prepare yourself, child," Maryam says. "You have no idea
what's in store for you."

I see their faces, sympathetic, worn, and beautiful. They
will help. They know what it is like to be desperate to change.

13

Katayoun agreed to meet me for lunch at Restaurant Javan. I've been waiting for her for a half hour, and I'm getting worried. The wedding is a month away, and nothing has changed. Reza is still handsome. Nasrin is still in denial. And Mrs. Mehdi is still fixing up her father's estate for the wedding. Nasrin's grandfather has a huge house with a big basement. The plan is to turn the basement into a subterranean dance party for the reception. I imagine it will be a tamer version of one of Ali's parties. Dariush is upset that he is not allowed to play DJ. Mrs. Mehdi has sense enough to limit her son's musical opportunities.

I asked the funny-looking man in the orange suit who runs the restaurant for a private table. He was more than accommodating, just like last time, but when he asked if Ali would be joining me, I lied and said he might show up. It's early enough that Ali is probably still in bed. At last Katayoun enters meekly, and I wave at her.

"Sorry to keep you waiting," she says, sitting down across from me. She glances around the room, a light sweat blooming on her upper lip.

"That's all right. Were you able to —?"

She answers by handing me a large paper bag. There it is, the start of my new life. I put the bag in my book bag and smile gratefully. "How much do I owe you?"

Katayoun shakes her head. "It's been paid for."

"Who . . . um, I mean, who paid, so I can properly thank them?"

"We all pitched in. Goli *khanum* and the rest of our group. Except for Maryam." I could die from embarrassment. Katayoun tells me how often I should take the drugs, explaining that I should insert the syringe in my thigh or my rear end. I should avoid veins, bones, and nerves. She emphasizes not to take more than I should, one cc a month. That gives me time for only one injection before the wedding. Maybe a beard will start to sprout, and Nasrin will see that I'm serious. It's scaring me a little.

"How long have you been taking them?" I ask as Katayoun continues to look around the room.

"A little over a year." Her eyes lock onto mine with a nervous intensity. "Why did you pick this place?" Her expression is like that of the cat I see by the schoolyard, skittish and fearful of everyone and everything nearby.

"I just thought you'd be more comfortable. There's a diverse crowd here, so — "

"*A diverse crowd?* Is that how you would put it?" Her tone has turned icy. Katayoun's face is scarlet, and her hands are clenched in fists on the table as if she is about to pound on it.

"It's safe to . . . Well, to be one's self in here. I mean, there is less of a chance of judgment or, I don't know, more of a chance for people who, I imagine, are sympathetic."

"I'm not like them! You hear me? What they do is unnatural." She whispers as her eyes train on a table of two men giving each other affectionate glances. It's the seething rage I don't understand. In meetings Katayoun is usually so demure and easily startled, especially when Maryam throws a verbal barb her way.

"I'm sorry. I just thought — "

"Thought what? That I am the same as these . . . these

perverts, just because I am different?" Some lady she turned out to be. She at least has the courtesy to whisper these hurtful things. They're hurtful because she's talking about me. I'm a pervert. Even if I change, my feelings for Nasrin have always been there.

"I thought by being someone who is different, you might sympathize with others who are also different." I don't want to argue with her. She was kind enough to bring me what I need, even if she is being an absolute bitch. Katayoun leans in, her face close to mine, and I can't will myself to move my head away for fear she might attack me.

"My illness is treatable. Their malady is a bargain made with the devil. The Republic knows that, the Koran knows that, and you damn well better know that if you are to survive in this society."

I slap Katayoun.

I should be apologetic. I'm not. I don't know where that came from—but it came, and a part of me is glad. My hand burns with shame as Katayoun begins to cry. Before I can apologize, she stands up and reaches for my book bag. She wants the hormones back. Like hell am I going to give them up. She beats her bony fists on my shoulders, calling me a liar and a degenerate. I grip my book bag tightly, blocking Katayoun with my body, though I'm still planted in my chair. Two servers arrive to break us up, but neither of them is allowed to touch us because we are women, so they waddle back and forth in between us like limping penguins. One of them tries to puff out his chest as big as he can to keep me from Katayoun, his hands behind his back.

"Give it back!" Katayoun shrieks. "You don't really want them! You're one of them," No! She's trying to take away my only hope. I slap her again with the back of my hand—I'll show her how manly I can be—and doing so feels good.

"Don't you dare judge me, you piece of trash." Oh my god—I said that out loud! Good! She had it coming. I clutch the book bag to my chest, hugging it like a life vest.

"What's all this?"

Oh no. Ali. He sounds so calm. I was stupid to think I wouldn't run into him, even though he's never out of his apartment this early. We should have met at Max Burger, but after the way Parveen was treated there, I didn't want Katayoun to face the same ugliness. I didn't expect her to be such a judgmental donkey butt.

"She took something of mine and won't give it back!"

Katayoun shrieks. Now she's accusing me of stealing. *Ajab gereftari*—what are the odds? When did this become my life?

"She did?" Ali turns to me. "Well, give it back. I'm sure I can buy you whatever junk this poor creature is peddling." He doesn't even defend me. He knows I would never steal.

"No. I need it." I'm not going to just roll over because he says so. He's used to people doing that, but I won't. This is none of his business! It's my body, my life, my love, and I will do with all of it what I can. Ali shoos away the two servers and the sad bald man in charge, all of whom have been hovering around the edges. They oblige and retreat, while others in the restaurant watch our display with great interest. I always manage to make a scene at this stupid place, with its cheap decor and mediocre food. Ali motions for Katayoun to sit. She refuses, shaking her head and with her arms folded across her chest.

Ali doesn't bat an eye. He sits across from me and extends his hand. "Whatever it is, I can get it for you in abundance. Just hand it back and she—I'm sorry, your name?" Ali asks smoothly, grinning at Katayoun in the way he has learned from the movies. He channels Fardin, an old, Persian movie star, and a bit of Cary Grant. He loves black-and-white movies.

I like some of them, too, but never watch them because Nasrin falls asleep.

"Katayoun," she says, calmer.

"Lovely. Won't you sit down?" He pulls over a chair from the next table. "I promise you what is owed you." He's actually flirting with her, and he's believable at that. She sits next to Ali. He smiles at her again before directing his attention toward me. "Now, what is it that you need so badly, Sahar?" I don't answer. He's getting annoyed. He turns back to Katayoun. She's melting under his gaze.

"I was delivering hormones for before her operation," Katayoun confesses. I shut my eyes. When I open them, Ali looks at me like I have just told him I have just killed Britney Spears, Madonna, and Lady Gaga.

Ali extends his hand again, but I refuse to hand him the bag. His jaw clenches. "Give it to me, Sahar. Or I will have you arrested."

"You wouldn't! You don't understand—"

"I understand perfectly." His tone is chilling and stirs such fear in me that I know he is serious. He has the power to do it. A call to Farshad, and I would be detained for a day, possibly beaten. I could risk prison. What's the worst they can do? I don't have much else to live for. I don't even study these days. I do my homework and take the tests, but it means nothing. I feel absolutely alone. "Give it to me, Sahar. We'll figure something out." I don't know if he's lying, but the way he says it reminds me of Maman. Damn him and his strong genes.

I plop my book bag on the table, and Katayoun rifles through it, procuring the coveted treasure. Ali just stares at me.

"You can go now." He raises his hand to shoo away Katayoun. She looks gutted and I'm glad, but I'm envious of her as she rushes out of the restaurant.

"You would really have me arrested?" I ask.

Ali leans back in his chair and purses his lips. "You would really be a man? What are you thinking?" I thought he would be supportive. He's so indifferent about what I do as it is, why should he care now? He gets whatever he wants. Why can't I get this one crucial thing? "It doesn't make everything go away. You will have to live in a body that isn't yours. A body that you don't belong in."

"It's legal this way," I whisper. Why can't he see that? I'm going to be free as a man. I'm going to live life fully for once.

He shakes his head. "She's not going to leave him. No matter what crazy thing you do."

That's not . . . He doesn't know that. I mean, she may just postpone the wedding or maybe Reza will fall down a cliff. The reality hits in a way it never has. I gasp. Everything is blurry. Ali motions a server for water. I drink, but it quenches nothing.

"Did Parveen put you up to it? Make it sound wonderful?" I shake my head. He pinches the bridge of his nose and takes a deep breath. "Nasrin . . . she likes you as you are. A male version of you would be perverse. It would frighten her."

No. I'm not going to give up. Even if it's wrong, there is still a chance, and that's more than I have as a woman. A chance. My only chance. I'm going to have that operation, and there's nothing anyone can do to stop me. I just have to figure out who is going to help me.

14

Baba is building a dresser for Nasrin and Reza. Mrs. Mehdi commissioned it, but I have a feeling it's more of a gift to my father than it is to her daughter. I'm grateful it gives him something to do, and he seems to enjoy his work again. It's a start. The past few nights he has stayed late at the workshop, and I have had the apartment to myself and my own thoughts. When I should be thinking about math equations and literature, I'm thinking about whether Parveen will help me. Even if my change isn't finished in time, maybe Nasrin won't go through with the wedding.

Nasrin will see me in the room, with peach fuzz growing from my chin, and she will stand up from the ceremony. She will topple over the *sofra,* all the elements before her: the pastries, flowers, candelabras, the cup of honey, the bowl of gold coins breaking. The mirror that the young couple is supposed to see themselves in will shatter, and we'll run away. A helicopter will be waiting for us to take us to Switzerland, where I will finally learn how to ski while Nasrin sits in a lodge eating chocolates. OK, none of that will happen, but if she knows I'm doing this, she will call off the wedding. She has to wait for me.

The intercom in our apartment buzzes. I'm not expecting anyone. I get up from the kitchen table, abandoning my books yet again, and push the intercom button. "Yes?"

"It's Parveen. May I come up?" I hesitate. After the debacle with Katayoun, I am sure word has gotten around that I am not who I presented myself to be. Parveen has been kind to me, though. I don't see why she would act differently now. I buzz her in and open the door, waiting for her to reach me at the top of the stairs. I can hear her high heels clack. I watch her from the doorway as she glides up the stairs. She is more of a woman than I will ever be. Being a woman comes naturally to her, effortlessly, and sometimes I wish I didn't know she is transsexual. It might make me feel better about my neglect of feminine pursuits. At least I wouldn't keep thinking about it when I speak with her.

"*Salam*, Sahar *joon*," Parveen says as she enters, kissing me on both cheeks. I lead her into the living room and wait for her to sit down. I offer her tea, but she declines. She can't stay for long. I sit down, waiting for a lecture or some kind of reproach for the way things happened at Restaurant Javan. Neither comes. Instead she asks me about the test and school. I'm grateful. Is it possible Katayoun didn't tell her? Our small talk continues for a while. We discuss the weather and how humid the days have become recently. Parveen even tells me a tame joke about a gorilla and tiger. I don't find it all that funny, but I laugh anyway.

"So, do you want to tell me why you really want to have the operation?" she asks at last.

I shouldn't be surprised, but I am caught off guard. My heart beats fast.

"As I said before, I feel like I am in the wrong—"

"It's okay, Sahar. I won't judge you. Just please don't lie to me or yourself anymore." I swallow down the fear that's been lodged in my throat for weeks.

"I suppose Katayoun told you."

"No. Your cousin called me. He sounded very concerned." She's waiting for me to explain myself, but I just can't. She clears her throat and goes in for the kill. "He mentioned a friend of yours getting married." My eyes snap wide. I could kill Ali. Parveen reaches over to take my hand in hers. "You didn't judge me, Sahar *joon*. I have no reason to judge you now."

I take a deep breath and apologize for deceiving her over and over again. I surprise myself by not crying. I don't explain the nature of my relationship with Nasrin, but I'm sure Ali has said more than he should. All I can tell her is that I thought my life would be easier as a man.

Parveen pats my hand and tells me I couldn't be more wrong. She tells me about Maryam and how Maryam, as a man, was in love with another man, which her older brother found out about. The brother was so angry, he threatened to turn Maryam into the police unless she changed from a man to a woman. Since her surgery, Maryam has become a heroin addict. She is always angry and has even attempted suicide. Goli *khanum* eventually took Maryam in to keep an eye on her, but Parveen wonders if some souls just can't be saved.

I've watched Maryam in meetings. The way she scoffs at others in the group and isolates herself made me think she just hates everybody else. I guess she hates herself . . . and maybe everyone else in the world, too.

"Do you want to end up like Maryam?" Parveen asks. "Bitter, depressed, and stuck?"

I know Parveen means well, but I have decided. "I know I'm not like you, and I'm sorry for pretending, but I can't turn away from this now. I will always wonder if . . . if she could love me if the circumstances were in our favor."

Parveen shakes her head and bites her lip. She thinks I'm incredibly stupid. I flush. She isn't wrong, but I always used to think I was so intelligent. Everyone told me I was. My parents, my teachers, my classmates, the Mehdis . . . Maybe Nasrin has been the smart one all along. She'll have a life of wealth, comfort, and privilege, and I will be left with nothing. Nasrin is all I care about—I don't have anyone else. I'm afraid of what my life will be like without her.

Parveen takes a deep breath and tries again. "I think this is a mistake for you, Sahar. You are not going to benefit from this the way a transsexual would. But you've made up your mind." I nod emphatically. It is what I want.

Isn't it?

"Is this girl worth it? I can't think much of a girl who would put you in this position, but is she really worth it? Have you discussed this with her? I can tell you, I have had people who don't accept me any longer because of my change. Relatives, friends, boyfriends—this is not an easy life. Will she accept you? Have you thought about all this?" Parveen is crying now, and I have never seen her do that before. She's always been so happy and confident. I embrace her and she folds into me, her tears dampening my shoulder. I don't let go until she is ready and backs away. She wipes her eyes and chuckles in embarrassment. "This life is not easy, but it's the one I wanted for myself. I just wish people would be more understanding. But you . . . You will be living a lie."

"I already am living a lie. What's another?"

Parveen takes in the statement and shakes her head. "Sahar, what you're thinking of doing is not right. I don't want you to regret this."

I'm tired of everyone looking at me like I am a delusional fool. I know what I'm doing! Kind of. "I'm going to do it, whether you help me or not. Who knows what will happen to me if you don't help me?"

And with that Parveen agrees to help. She says she will set up an appointment with her former surgeon, Dr. Hosseini, a few days from now. I will have to miss school, which I have never done before, but I am more than willing. I don't even care if Baba finds out. He hasn't noticed anything about me in the past few years, so I doubt he will know I have missed school. I doubt he would even notice if I came home as a boy. The appointment with the doctor is just a preliminary meeting, during which he will explain that there is no way I can have the surgery before the wedding. I don't care. Divorce is legal in Iran, and maybe by the time I have a handle on being a man Nasrin will realize her marriage is a farce—and we can be together. Wouldn't that be incredible?

The buzzer sounds again, and I get up to check the intercom. There's only one person it could be. I stand up and push the button to speak.

"*Baleh?*" I ask.

"Sahar! Let me up! I'm dying to see you." I look over at Parveen, who stares at the floor. I shouldn't let her up, but I've never denied her anything before. I push the button, unlocking the door, and greet Nasrin when she enters.

"It's so hot out! I thought I might faint." Nasrin laughs, but her smile fades when she sees Parveen. "Sorry, I didn't know you have company." I take Nasrin's hand and drag her into the living room. I introduce the two, and Parveen stands, gracious and polite as ever, and kisses Nasrin on both cheeks.

Nasrin goes through the motions, but I can already tell she is assessing Parveen's looks.

"Nasrin is getting married soon," I tell Parveen, and she doesn't blink an eye. She knew exactly who this was. Parveen congratulates Nasrin, who thanks her, but there's an obvious tension in the room. I shouldn't have let Nasrin up. Parveen quickly says she has an appointment to go to but adds that she wishes Nasrin all the best. I hug her, and thank her, and I can feel Nasrin's eyes on the back of my neck. When Parveen leaves I close the door behind her and turn to Nasrin.

"How do you know her?" she asks.

"She's a friend of mine. She's helping me with something important." I think about what Parveen has said, about how I should talk with Nasrin about what I plan to do.

"She's pretty," Nasrin says. She looks annoyed, but on her, jealousy is adorable. "What's she helping you with?"

"A way to stop the wedding," I say. She doesn't comment on that. "I like when you're jealous, Nasrin. It makes you know what it feels like to be me."

I go to the kitchen to brew tea while Nasrin slumps on the living room couch. She tells me about the new drama at the Mehdi household: Sima, the daughter of Soraya, the maid, came to ask for Dariush's hand in marriage! It's unusual for a woman to ask for a man's hand in marriage, but Sima was always one of a kind. Mrs. Mehdi laughed, though Mr. Mehdi actually heard her out and didn't think it would be such a bad idea. Sima will eventually be a pharmacist, and she will make a good living. Nasrin laughs, explaining how Dariush just sat there like a limp piece of fish, his mouth flapping open and then shut and then open again.

"Will your family have another wedding on its hands?" I ask as I pour Nasrin's tea in front of her, putting three sugar cubes on her plate to sweeten it, just the way she likes it. Nasrin has such a sweet tooth, I am shocked her teeth have not fallen out.

Nasrin laughs at me as though I am a fool. "Of course not! My mother was so outraged at the idea of her servant's daughter having the gall to ask, she kicked her out. Now Sima is moving her mother out of the house to go live with her." Nasrin takes a sip of tea. "It's a pity. Soraya is an amazing cook," she adds as an afterthought.

My stomach sinks when I think of Sima leaving the Mehdi house, dejected and broken at the hands of Mrs. Mehdi after being so brave and full of hope. "Sima is beautiful and smart.

Why wouldn't Dariush marry her?" I know why Mrs. Mehdi wouldn't allow it, but Sima has a better station in life than Dariush could expect without his parents' wealth. It's likely she would work all day and come home to a lounging Dariush playing the same three chords on his out-of-tune guitar.

Nasrin lowers her teacup and gives me an incredulous look. "Can you imagine the bride's side of the family? Arriving at the wedding with their toothless grins and shuffling feet, trying to dance? How embarrassing." Now she's laughing again. She enjoyed that scenario a little too much. I'm still silent, and she can tell I'm angry, because her smirk dissolves and she clears her throat. This isn't the Nasrin I know.

"That was an awful thing to say."

"Sahar, *shookhi mikonam*—I'm joking! I do have to give Sima credit for having courage. That was not an easy task, facing my mother and father. But it never would have worked between them. They come from different classes. If Dariush had wanted to marry her, he would have done something about it."

My *maman* married my baba even though they were of different classes. Maman was brave that way. "Dariush is afraid of disappointing your parents and losing his inheritance," I tell her, and she rolls her eyes at me. She looks a little ugly.

"He's already disappointed my parents. He doesn't want to have to work for Sima. She won't let him just sit around all day. He'll have to cook and clean or start working more at the garage. Do you think he wants that kind of life? I don't care how he feels about her; he's never going to make his life harder than it has to be."

And neither are you. It's all very clear now.

I excuse myself and go to the bathroom. I wash my face with cool water, trying to calm down after Nasrin's antics. I stare at myself in the mirror for a long time. I notice the pimple that wants to poke through on my chin. I notice the scar on my eyebrow from roller-skating down a slide at a playground years ago. Nasrin had dared me to do it. It's a small scar, but at age seven Nasrin had rushed to my side and cried over my cut. I was more shocked and didn't cry at all. She felt guilty after that, and we didn't play as much outside. She was protective of me then. That doesn't seem to be the case anymore.

"Sahar, what are you doing in there? Are you constipated?" Nasrin likes to bring up my past maladies. I open the door, and she looks at me with warmth. "I'm sorry about what I said. You know I love Soraya, and I think Sima . . . Well, I never did like how you two got along so well. So maybe I was happy she didn't get what she wanted."

"If I was a man, would you marry me? Even if I wasn't rich and couldn't give you everything Reza could right away. I would eventually, but would you marry me?" There isn't any of the pleading she's used to in my voice. It's a clear, determined question, one that I hope she answers honestly.

"Why are you so obsessed with marriage? I hardly want to marry Reza, who is actually so sweet I might go crazy. Do you know what it's like to be around a perfect person? It's exhausting. I'm just waiting for some big, dark secret to come out—like he's from another planet or he's a robot." She's not taking me seriously. She is deflecting my question, and I don't have time for that anymore. I grab her roughly by her shoulders. She doesn't look scared. She knows I would never hurt her. Maybe I want her to be a little scared.

"I need an answer from you. Please don't treat me like I'm some silly girl, because we're too old for that now. If I were a man, would you be with me? Would you leave him for me?"

Nasrin hesitates, but I'm giving her time to really think about the question. I don't want her to give me a rushed answer she thinks I want to hear. She shrugs against my hands, and I let go of her. She grazes my cheek with her finger and traces my lips, my chin, and my eyebrows. She twirls a tendril of my hair around her finger. I don't melt under her touch like I always do. I'm going to remain vigilant.

"You wouldn't look so bad with a beard." She grins. It's all the answer I need.

15

Parveen is waiting for me in front of the Mirdamad Sur-
gical Centre. She doesn't see me at first. She is tugging at her
sleeves; I thought I was supposed to be the nervous one. A
masculine woman with thick glasses and unplucked facial hair
walks into the clinic. I am really here. I am really doing this.

"I'm sorry, my taxi got stuck in traffic," I say, and Parveen
launches into my arms, giving me a tight hug.

"This isn't who you are. Please don't do this," she whispers,
and I go limp in her arms. I can feel her tears on my neck. The
tenderness reminds me of my *maman*. I push away from her.

"You promised you would help me. I have to do this, or I
will lose her." I whisper my plea to her, so that passersby can't
hear us. Parveen wipes at her eyes, which are the greenest they
have ever been. She nods and turns to walk into the clinic. I

follow her as she checks in at the front desk. The attendant recognizes Parveen and asks how her family is. We get a number, like we are waiting for a kabob order.

There are other patients. A little girl, about three years old with a cleft palate lip and a Hello Kitty bow in her hair. There is a man in his forties, with steely eyes and no legs. He probably served in the war when he was my age. Maman used to tell stories about how she and her family would hide in the basement, waiting for the bombs to come. Sometimes the bombs came, sometimes they didn't. It was a waiting game.

I haven't been to a hospital since Maman died. She was hooked up to tubes to help her breathe. I thought she would get better. If she could survive a war unscathed, surely she could survive a mere heart condition. I suppose the heart always betrays us one way or another.

"The doctor is very nice." Parveen says. "If you have any questions, let him know immediately." Nasrin was at the hospital with me when Maman passed. She didn't know what to do, whether she should leave me alone or coo over me. She held my hand the whole time. The sweat on her palm blended with mine. Baba cried while the Mehdis tried to comfort him.

Neither Nasrin nor I cried. We were being brave for each other. I am being brave for her now.

"How long ago did you, um . . . did you have your operation?" I ask.

"It's been five years," Parveen immediately answers.

"Did it hurt?" I know it did. I don't know why I'm asking.

"Yes, more than you can imagine," Parveen says. The little girl with the cleft palette stares at me. I smile at her because somebody should. She does the same back, her gums exposed, her nose flaring more than those of other little girls. The little girl's mother is in a full *chador*, her black eyes peering out of her tent. Maybe I can pretend Maman is underneath all that cloth, making sure everything will be fine. Though Maman would never wear a full *chador*.

Parveen taps her fingers on the arm of her chair. I want to ask her to stop, but that would be rude. This is more her place than mine. So many transsexuals come up to her while we are in the waiting room. She smiles like a beauty queen, and I wonder how many people she has helped with this. I haven't helped anyone with anything. I'm selfish. Parveen doesn't introduce me to the patients and their families. I don't think she wants to admit to herself, or to anyone else, why we are here.

A man dressed in women's clothing approaches us with his mother beside him. He asks Parveen to explain to his mother that this isn't a choice. Parveen gives the speech that I have heard countless times in meetings. I look over to my left, and the doctor's office door is open. A man with white hair sits behind a desk. He looks kind. I hope he is my doctor. He's talking to someone standing next to his desk, a man, but I can't see his face. The man is wearing a lab coat. He turns around. My nails dig into Parveen's hand, and she lets out a yelp.

The man in the lab coat is Reza. I have to get out of here. How on Allah's green earth is this possible? Another cruel joke being thrown my way.

"*Shomare* 137, number 137," comes over the loudspeaker. It's our number! I'm going to be sick.

"Ow!" Parveen cries, and the women who have been talking to her look at me like I'm crazy. Does Nasrin know he's this kind of surgeon? Why didn't she tell me? I tie my head scarf tight around my head, hiding as much of my face as possible. My nose and eyes are all that poke out. Oh god, he's going to recognize me! The little girl with the cleft palate laughs at me, thinking my erratic behavior is a part of some game. The women nod politely at Parveen and back away slowly.

"Do you have a *hijab*?" I ask Parveen. She opens her purse and pulls out her *chador,* for when she goes to the mosque. I wrap it around myself and hide my face. It's the only time in my life a *hijab* has come in handy.

"What are you doing?" Parveen asks, but I can't answer. We both look into the office, and Reza comes into the waiting area, calling out Parveen's name from his clipboard. I cling to Parveen's hand.

"That's Nasrin's fiancé," I say. Parveen stiffens and looks with wide eyes at the doctor. Reza doesn't recognize me; he just gives us a goofy smile. I have to get out of here.

"We can leave," Parveen says. But this is my time to meet with the doctor. Who knows when I will get another chance? I don't want the doctor to think I'm not serious about doing this and blacklist me so that I will never get another appointment.

"No. I have to do this. He doesn't recognize me. But I need to get rid of him." Dr. Hosseini stands from behind his desk and nods at Parveen and me. Reza closes the door behind us. I'm trapped!

"Thank you for meeting with us on such short notice, Dr. Hosseini," Parveen says as she sits down. I stay standing. I feel like I am going to hyperventilate. I don't know what to do.

"My dear, you may sit down, if you please," Dr. Hosseini says. I am silent, glued to the floor where I am standing, and Parveen looks up at me in embarrassment.

"Is something the matter?" Dr. Hosseini asks. Yes. I really wish the linoleum floor would open up and swallow me whole. I could land in hell in no time, Angry Grandpa scolding me on my way down.

"Dr. Hosseini, my friend . . . She, well, it's embarrassing, but she's afraid your young attendant keeps looking at her," Parveen says, and I blush furiously under my chador.

"Oh no! Dr. Hosseini, I haven't been! I'm getting married, sir! I would never." God, he's even nice when he's being wrongly accused. Dr. Hosseini just waves his hands at Reza.

"It's all right, Mahdavi. If it makes the young lady more comfortable, could you wait outside?" It worked! Thank you, Allah, you're the best!

"Of course, sir. I'm so sorry if she felt that way. I wasn't, honestly. I'm truly sorry . . ." Reza keeps apologizing as he exits the office. That's right, Mr. Perfect. No one wants you here. I sit down, across from the doctor.

"Now, how can I help you, my dear?" Dr. Hosseini asks

warmly. He doesn't look like a bad person. I'm still not going to show him my face. He only gets to see my eyes.

"Well, sir, you see, I was hoping you could turn me into a man," I say. I mean, why else would I be here? I don't say that bit out loud. Dr. Hosseini leans forward in his leather chair, and I can't help but lean forward in mine. He takes off his glasses and pinches the bridge of his nose. My *maman* used to do that when she was annoyed.

"Before we get started, I need you to be absolutely sure that this is something you want. So I will say my piece, and I don't want you to interrupt until I have finished. Okay?" I nod. Parveen inhales deeply. I wonder how many times she has had to hear him give this lecture and whether or not it's a flashback to her own first time in his office. "This operation, that we are discussing, is from hell. Your friend sitting next to you can attest to that." He motions to Parveen and her face goes pale. "Do you remember the agony you were in? We ripped your body apart, and stitched you back up, and the week of pain afterward . . . Would you wish that upon your worst enemy?" Parveen shakes her head and begins to cry. Oh no. This is so terribly awkward. Well, I'm doing it. I don't care what the man has to say.

"After the surgery, you can never conceive a child of your own. You may want to marry someday, and a family will not be an option for you. You may not know it yet, but adoption will be very difficult given your transsexual status. Do you understand?"

I know the basic biology of things. I'm not an idiot. I don't know if I want children. It isn't something I have ever thought about. The idea of being a parent scares me, because I know what it's like when your parents abandon you, unintentionally or not. If I had a child and something ever happened to me, I'd never forgive myself. Mrs. Mehdi's voice telling me how much Nasrin loves children pops into my head.

" Now, the chest reconstruction, the way we handle that . . ." Dr. Hosseini says. Immediately my nipples are at full attention, and I'm so glad this *chador* is hiding them. Fine, so my nipples don't want this to happen, either. But who asked them? "There will probably be some scarring, and your nipples will be grafted on. I have a photograph here of what that might look like." He shows me the photograph and my nipples are peaking, begging me to call this off. I look over at Parveen, who is still pale and remembering the pain of her own operation. "If you would like your vaginal opening closed, we will perform a vaginectomy, which is the removal of your vagina. You then could consider having a phalloplasty, which is the construction of a penis." As he keeps talking, I cross my legs. My vagina is not happy with this plan.

Dr. Hosseini continues to discuss skin he can take from various parts of my body to help construct a penis. Skin from my calf will allow me erotic sensation, while skin from my abdominal flap won't. Then he says that some patients prefer a metoidioplasty. This involves gradually filling my clitoris with testosterone, then releasing the clitoral hood . . . Something about increasing organ length and moving it forward . . . This allows sensation, whereas a phalloplasty . . . Something about lengthening the urethra . . . God, those diagrams are graphic. I clench my thighs tighter together. He goes on about the hormone therapy I will have to undergo, how to inject the drugs, the blood work, the psychiatrist I will have to visit for six months, and I—

I'm on the floor, flat on my back, with Dr. Hosseini and Parveen hovering over me.

"Sahar, are you okay?" Parveen asks, eyes full of concern. The doctor explains that I fainted. He tells me to sit up slowly, and Parveen helps me to a seated position. She flops her *chador* around me, hiding my face from the doctor. Dr. Hosseini hands me a cup of water while I remain on the floor. I sip from it, and I can't even look him in the face.

"That wasn't meant to scare you," he says. "It's just the way this process happens. You have to be sure this is something you want." I think about how I am letting myself down. How can I be the way I am and live in Iran? I look up, and there are two framed photographs, Angry Grandpa and Disappointed Grandpa. I swear Angry Grandpa is smirking. Disappointed Grandpa just looks at me like he knew I couldn't do it. He knew I wasn't brave enough.

"I'm sorry to make such a scene. I . . . I don't think," I say.

Reza rushes in with a cup of water. He recognizes me now. I could die.

"Sahar? What are you . . .?" He is speechless for a moment. He can see the fear in my eyes, and he knows why I'm here. *I want to be like you.* I hope he doesn't know why I want to be like him. His mouth is open, but slowly, remembering where he is, he crouches down and hands me the cup of water. "Does your father know you're here?" he asks. The jig is up. I start to cry. Parveen holds me. The doctor tells me everything will be fine. I thought I could do it. Now what will I do?

16

My school called Baba to see why I was absent yesterday and he's been trying to get an answer from me. It's too bad I'm lying in a fetal position on my bed and don't feel like talking to anyone. He should understand that. He's been doing more or less the same thing since Maman died. He bought some ready-made *khoreshts,* stews, in cans from the corner store by our apartment. I would be impressed except for the fact that I am absolutely devastated that this wedding is happening, and I cannot stop it. No more wild fantasies, no more attempts at making this atrocity go away. It's happening.

I don't know if Reza told Nasrin that he saw me at the clinic. I don't know what he thinks or if he suspects anything about Nasrin and me. I can't get the surgery now because Reza would know. Parveen dropped me off at home, after my fainting at the doctor's. She didn't stay long, said she had to get back to work at the bank. Parveen did give me a hug and told me everything would be fine. I felt like she was lying, but it was a nice gesture, anyway. Ali hasn't called me. He is probably still angry about my making a spectacle of myself at the restaurant. It doesn't matter. I don't need anybody.

"Sahar, can I come in?" Baba calls through the door to my room. I do not answer him. To my surprise, he actually comes in anyway. "Sahar *joon,* come have something to eat. I have *fesenjoon.* And *noon sangak,* you love warm bread." I keep my back to him. I am staring at photographs of Nasrin, taken on my fifth birthday, hanging on the wall next to my bed. In one of them Maman is hugging me from behind, and Nasrin is smearing frosting on her brother Cyrus's face.

Baba sits on my bed and touches my shoulder. "Your teacher said your grades have gotten worse. I didn't know what to tell her. Your grades have always been excellent. Even in preschool you were obsessed with knowing the right words to nursery rhymes." I don't care if he's disappointed. Maybe I figured out there is no point to schoolwork. I'll still be a huge lesbian without a girlfriend. He lets go of my shoulder. Good. I hope he's finished.

"Should I call Nasrin to come over?"

I start hysterically laughing. I sit up and look at him. He is so confused. He knows exactly who I've always needed in times like this. But he can't know that right now, Nasrin might be the last person I want to see. I'm starting to cry from laughing so hard, and Baba looks concerned.

"Call Nasrin?" I ask. "Do you want to know why my grades are suffering? Why I skipped school? Why everything has stopped making sense?" I want him to know. I want him to know me, to know what I have painfully and silently been dealing with. "Do you want to know what Nasrin does when she comes over here that makes me feel so good?" Won't he be surprised to know his daughter is an enemy of the state, a lowlife, and an aberration from God's plan.

"She listens to you?"

The anger leaves me. He looks so helpless and innocent, like a sheep that's about to be slaughtered for the end of Ramadan.

Maybe that *is* why I am so devoted to her. She listens to me.

For all of her self-centered activities and vanity, when I speak Nasrin listens. She lets me talk when society and the rest of the world won't. She's heard my inner voice, and she still loves me. Maybe Baba isn't the stranger I thought he was.

"Yes. She listens to me. I . . . thank you for buying dinner." Baba sits there, patient and waiting for more of an explanation. It's hard to be mad at him. He's just so clueless. "I'm just sad that I am losing Nasrin. That she's getting married." That's about as close as I will ever come to telling him the truth. I don't want him to worry about me. I don't want him to get in trouble or monitor everywhere I go. It's like Maman said, it's better to leave thoughts of marrying Nasrin alone.

"Sahar *joon,* don't be upset. Just because she is getting married doesn't mean Nasrin doesn't love you. You can still visit, and she can come here anytime. Her husband can come, too, if he likes. We can make them dinner together." It's more than I expected him to say. It doesn't make me feel better, but at least he's trying. "Besides, when you go to university you won't have time to cook, and it's about time I learned. If you have some time, you could teach me." University. There is still that. I could be a better doctor than Reza. Maybe I could be a cardiologist and spare other little girls the pain of losing a parent to heart failure. I still have a life to live, even if Nasrin isn't a part of it.

"Yes. I'd like that," I tell him, and he smiles. It breaks my heart because I haven't seen him smile like that in such a long time.

"My rice is even edible tonight. You should try it. I shocked myself." Now it's my turn to smile. He's trying, like I have asked him to. Baba leads me into the kitchen and tells me to call Ali to join us. I might as well. I have yet to apologize for the scene I made. I call Ali's mobile, but there is no answer. I call his apartment. No answer. He's probably out with friends. Of course he's with friends; he's always with friends. He has thousands of friends, and I am forever friendless and having dinner with my father.

"I think it's just us tonight," I say, and plop down into a kitchen chair. I'm not going to set the table. I'm not going to serve the food. I'm not going to do anything. Baba seems fine with that as he turns on the TV to the football match. Neither of us likes football; it's the noise that we enjoy. It covers up our awkward silence. Baba puts down a plate of semiburnt rice with *fesenjoon* on top. *Fesenjoon* has always looked like diarrhea to me. It's a pomegranate stew with chopped walnuts and chicken in it. It tastes delicious, if you have a blindfold on.

There's a buzz at the door. Baba and I look at each other

in confusion. He stands up and pushes the intercom button. *"Baleh?"*

"Dayi, let me in!" It's Ali and he sounds drunk.

I rush to the door and usurp Baba at the intercom.

"Ali, what do you want?" He has such nerve to come here in that state. A young girl's voice comes over the intercom. It's Daughter.

"Please, let us up? He's been hurt. We don't know what to do." I immediately hit the buzzer. I know Ali enough to understand that he would never bring Daughter here unless it was an absolute emergency. I open the door and see Ali, one arm slung over Mother's shoulder, the other over Daughter's. His face looks like it has bits of smashed pomegranate all over. His lip is bleeding, and he has a swollen eye. Baba rushes to support Ali and guide him into the apartment. Baba sits him down on a sofa. Daughter is breathing heavily. Mother coolly takes off her gloves.

"What happened?" I ask, and Baba looks at me, just as bewildered. Daughter begins to cry a little bit.

"I think you'd better wash him up first," Mother says. "He might bleed on your furniture." I've never liked this bitch. I rush to the bathroom and wet a towel. Daughter is now wailing in the living room. I rush back to the sofa. Ali looks so small as I gently pat his face.

"Should we take him to a hospital?" Baba asks.

"No!" All four of us shout.

Ali winces, and I know whatever trouble he's in, there's a reason he's here. He has nowhere else to hide. I press the towel on his bad eye.

"Baba, hold the towel here. I'll call for help."

"Who are you calling?" Baba asks. The last person in the world I would ever want to call. Ali owes me, big time. I walk to my room and dial on my mobile. The phone rings twice before Nasrin picks up.

"*Salam, azizam!* My parents are out to eat if you want to come over and—"

"I need Reza. Ali's been hurt, and he needs a doctor," I mutter through gritted teeth. I can hear her gasp. She knows it must be serious because there is no other reason I would sacrifice making out with her. There's no other reason why I would ask for her stupidly perfect fiancé to come over to my home.

"He's . . . I think he's at the hospital. I'll have him paged. He should be finished soon."

"Please tell him to hurry."

"Of course! Do you want me to come over?"

"No! No, it's . . . Don't worry."

"Okay." We breathe in and out at the same time.

"I can't . . . I couldn't find a way to stop the wedding," I say and she sighs into the phone.

"It's all right. What could you have done?"

"I have to go."

"All right, I love y —"

I hang up on her. I walk back into the living room. I turn to Ali. His bleeding seems to have stopped, but Baba keeps the towel on him. Mother has made herself comfortable at the kitchen table. Daughter still stands, her hands shaking. She can't stop crying, and I stand next to her, rubbing my hand on her back to try to soothe her.

"It's all right. Shhh. He will be fine, he's always fine." I say it for the benefit of both of us. I look over my shoulder at Ali. He doesn't seem all that badly injured, but he looks like hell. I lead Daughter to sit across from Mother at the kitchen table.

"What happened?" I whisper to Mother. I don't want Baba to know what Ali has been up to.

"May we have some tea first? It's not easy hauling a man up the stairs. Even if he is terribly skinny." I slam my fist down on the table. Daughter whimpers, and Baba looks over, alarmed.

"Sahar? What's going on?" he asks, and I wish he weren't home now.

"Nothing! Just getting some tea," I say. Mother just smirks. I go to the cupboard, pull out two tea glasses, and pour some *chai* for our visitors. I drop Mother's in front of her, splashing tea onto the table. I gently hand a glass to Daughter, pressing it into her still shaking hands. "No sugar?" Mother asks.

"No sugar. What happened?"

Mother raises an eyebrow and finally concedes to tell me. "We were in the middle of a *negotiation*, and he called us to pick him up. He sounded strange, and when he told us where to find him, I thought he was joking." I look at Ali.

"*Natars, dayi jan*," Ali says. "I just had a disagreement with someone. I'll be fine." He's calling to me, but he's smiling at Baba's sad, worried face, trying to convince him not to worry.

"Where did you pick him up?" I ask.

"The police station," Daughter says. They finally caught him. Invincible Ali. Bruised and battered on his dead aunt's couch.

"He was on the curb when we pulled up. He had the courtesy to make sure we didn't have to go inside. This one was scared out of her mind." Mother nods at Daughter.

"I've never been arrested," Daughter says, and I put my hand over her shaking ones. "I've heard stories of what happens. Just stories, but you never know."

The phone rings and I dart over to answer it. *"Baleh?* Hello?"

"Sahar? It's Reza. Nasrin said your cousin is hurt?"

"Yes. He's conscious; he's been beaten. He needs some cleaning up, and I don't know —"

"It's all right. I will be there shortly. I'm driving over right now." He doesn't mention anything about seeing me at the clinic. I hate that he's so nice. He and I could have been friends, maybe colleagues one day.

"Thank you" is all I can muster.

"It's fine. Nasrin would kill me if I didn't help you. You should have heard her on the phone." I smile at that. She can get into such a mood.

"Just make sure he stays conscious." He hangs up, and I'm sure Nasrin has told him not to ask any questions. I hang up the phone, and I crouch down next to Baba and take over holding the towel on Ali's face. Baba starts to cry and Ali rolls his eyes.

"Can you tell him to stop that? I'm fine!" Ali says. If his face didn't look like a busted prune already, I would slap him.

"Baba, I made some tea and we have company. Go sit with them until Reza arrives."

Ali chuckles when he and I are alone. "Do I look tough, though? Boys really like that. You know, like a Clint Eastwood type. I always thought Marlon Brando was better looking. Even when he got fat." I don't know what he's talking about.

"Just shut up, Ali. Can you do that for once? Shut up?"

"Sahar, you're going to get frown lines if you keep looking at me like that. No one wants a girl with frown lines."

"What are you going to do?" I ask.

Ali looks at me like a kid who has been asked what he would like for his birthday. He thinks for a long moment, then shrugs. "Run," he says.

I haven't asked who has beaten him like this, but whoever it was, they know about Ali. They know what he does, where he does it, who his friends are, which coffee shops are notorious, and when he will be there. They know who he is. He has signed off on his own death sentence. There is no place in Iran for Ali any longer.

The buzzer sounds and Baba answers, greeting Reza at the door. Reza rushes to us, inspecting Ali. He *is* Superman! He puts on latex gloves and gets to work assessing Ali's wounds. Reza pulls materials from his magic doctor bag and washes all the cuts. He asks Ali where he was hit, if he hurts anywhere else.

Ali admits he was punched several times, in the torso, and kicked in the groin. His hand was smashed under a boot, and he received some lashings on his back.

"Can we go now?" Mother asks Ali coldly from the kitchen. Ali gives her a wink and she rolls her eyes. Daughter comes over to Ali and kisses his hand. She starts crying again.

"Don't do that, *azizam*. Shhh, I'm fine! I'll see you soon." The way Ali says it, I don't think he will.

Daughter keeps crying, and I stand up, clutch her shoulders, and walk her over to Mother.

"What's your name?" I whisper in her ear. She stops her tears for a moment and smiles. I don't think she gets asked that very often.

"Nastaran. My name is Nastaran."

"That's a beautiful name. I'm Sahar. You can always come

here if you need a place," I say, not caring about the consequences. She hugs me tight. I think Maman would be proud of me. When Nastaran lets me go, she runs down the stairs to her waiting pimp. I hope I see her again. I really do.

"I think you should still visit a hospital, if you can," Reza says to Ali. "I'm not sure if you sustained any internal injuries." Unfortunately, there is no X-ray machine in Reza's bag of wonders.

"I'm fine. I'll be fine," Ali says. I think that is the best we are going to get out of him tonight. He reaches into his jeans pocket and pulls out a crumpled wad of bills. The good doctor politely shakes his head and bids his patient good night.

"Thank you for coming," I say. "I know this must all seem very strange."

"It's none of my business, Sahar," Reza says pointedly, and I can tell he isn't just talking about Ali. Does he know why I was going to have the surgery? I can't tell. "I'm just happy to help," Reza adds. "He should be fine, but call me anytime if he's in critical pain." I should let him know that his wife is no good for him. He can do better. He deserves better.

"I'm sorry," I say, and it's all I have to offer him.

17

ALI HAS BEEN STAYING with us for two weeks now. Farshad, the hulking police officer, finally asked for something Ali wouldn't give him: Parveen. Not that Ali has any ownership over her, but I know if Ali asked her, she would have entertained the idea. Ali said no.

"Farshad didn't like my answer," Ali joked. Farshad and his associates picked Ali up from the park and arrested him for possessing contraband items. Ali says the drugs were planted on him, but I think Ali is arrogant enough to feel like he can get away with anything. The officers gave him hell. They forced Ali to stand for two days, beating him to a pulp afterward.

Baba is nervous, and asks Ali what he plans on doing. It's his polite way of telling Ali he can't stay here. Baba's terrified of the police. Baba's terrified for *me*.

Parveen runs errands for Ali. She cried when she saw him all bruised and battered. "Stop acting like a baby," Ali said to her. I wanted to bruise him more after he said that. She secretly brings things he needs from his apartment over to ours. His shoe collection alone fills up most of my bedroom. When I come home from school Ali is always on the phone, arranging his business affairs, trying to sell his apartment, doing all manner of things to get out as fast as he can. Ali has decided to run away to Turkey. He hasn't told his parents yet. I don't think he plans on telling them until he has left the country.

Ali has hooked our apartment up to the neighbor's illegal satellite. Now he watches all the music videos he wants. Jennifer Lopez is his favorite. He mimics shaking his skinny butt like she does, with a cigarette dangling from his scabbed lips.

"You're really going to leave?" I ask as he jiggles his hips with his arms spread wide open. With the scars on his face, it makes him look like a gay Jesus.

"Yes, Sahar. Or have you been oblivious to this past week?" He's being a, pardon my language, asshole. I suppose losing everything in your sad little empire will do that to a person. I sit down in Baba's armchair. The next music video is a Persian singer from Los Angeles. He isn't very attractive and his voice sounds like crap. I imagine he was studying to be an engineer, failed his exams, and decided to become a singer instead. I imagine people have the luxury of doing that kind of thing in the West.

"How are you going to get there?" I ask. Ali sighs. I think it's a fair question.

"Mother is going to drive me as far as Karaj. I will stay with an old friend there, who will take me to Tabriz. I'll say good-bye to my parents, maybe stay there a few days, and then it's off to the border." I bet he doesn't make it. He doesn't do well with hardship. "Do you want to come with me?" I just blink at him. I must have not heard him correctly.

"What?"

"Do. You. Want. To. Come with me?" he says as he sits down on the sofa. He's crazy. Go with him? Leave Iran forever like some fugitive in the night? He rolls his eyes. "What are your reasons to stay, Sahar?"

"I—I have school, and—"

"Right, but what if you don't do well on the university entrance exam? There's always that possibility. They'll decide what future you should have. Maybe you'll end up being an accountant, a fate worse than death." He shudders. I haven't been focused on my studies lately. That's partially Ali's fault.

"I couldn't leave Baba." As soon as I say it, Ali chuckles cruelly.

"You're staying to be his maid? Do you plan on cooking for him for the rest of your life?" But Baba needs me. I'm all he has left. Then again, I can't look after him forever. Maman wouldn't like that.

"I don't speak much Turkish," I say, and Ali knows I'm stalling now.

"You're clever. We'd pick up the local slang in no time. We can go dancing! You wouldn't have to wear all those rags on your head in this scorching heat. You can drink in the open. No one can tell you what to do or how to think. There are even gay nightclubs! You could find a nice girlfriend with big breasts! We can be free. Can you imagine?"

"I can't leave Nasrin." That is the truth of my existence. I could never leave Nasrin. Even if she's leaving me, I can't leave her. Ali just takes a slow drag of his cigarette before putting it out in an ashtray with Saddam Hussein's face inside. The kind of merchandise Ali had been selling.

"You're sad, you know that? You obsess over that spoiled girl because you don't know anything else. Do you think she'd miss you if you left tomorrow? All you are to her is a stray cat following her around. She just needs to pet you a few times and you're satisfied." It's not true. She loves me. I know she does. He knows she does. "She's marrying the good doctor and she doesn't want you to stop her. Don't you understand? She is leaving you behind and she's happy to be rid of you."

I leap onto Ali from the chair and beat my fists on his chest.

"You *ahmag*! Just because you don't know how to love anyone, you have to make me feel like dirt." I start hitting his face and he squeals like a little girl. He pulls my hair and I keep lunging, smacking his already bruised face. He pushes me off and I land on the floor, breathless and sweaty. Ali leans over me and grabs the collar of my shirt. "I'm just trying to let you see things as they are, Sahar. If she doesn't want you, I could use a travel companion. I want you in my life, even if no one else does." He lets go and leaves me on the ground. I hear him open the refrigerator door, probably getting ice for his face. I don't get up to look. My cell phone rings in my jeans pocket. It's Nasrin's ring tone. What does she want now?

"Answer it," Ali says. "Your precious, spoiled brat is calling you." I run to my room. Foolish girl that I am, I answer the phone.

"Come downstairs!" Nasrin coos.

"What? I can't, I have homework and—"

"I miss you. Come down." I think about what Ali has said. How I mean nothing to her. Maybe I should leave with him. This afternoon might help me decide.

"I can't be out too long," I say. I definitely hear her chuckle. We both know it isn't up to me what time I get home.

"Just come down, Sahar *joon*. And slap your idiot cousin upside the head before you leave," she says before she hangs up.

I don't even check how I look in the mirror before I exit my room. My idiot cousin—he does foolish things, but he's not stupid. He sees things as they are. No, she loves me. Yes. She has to after all this time. But it's ending; the wedding is happening in a week, and she didn't even try. She didn't even mention stopping it. Not once. Ali sits on the couch, watching the unfortunate pop singer from Los Angeles.

"When are you leaving?' I ask him.

He smiles. "Right before her wedding. I think that's as good a time as any."

"It is." I nod and put on my head scarf and coat.

"You aren't going to keep her waiting?" Ali says, and my anger dissipates. He just doesn't want to see me be a fool, as I have been.

"This is the last time," I say. "She'll belong to someone else soon enough." I love her, but it's all too dangerous now. Adultery and homosexuality are two things the law won't abide. I don't want to hang like those boys in the square, and I don't want that for Nasrin.

This can be our good-bye.

When I exit the apartment building, she's waiting for me in a taxicab. Gazing through the window, I see she looks as beautiful as ever, her hair cascading out of her scarf and those lips that curve to the side when she is deep in thought. I enter the taxi and she smiles at me, like she knows some secret that I will never figure out. I probably never will. Nasrin puts her hand on mine.

"Where are we going?" I ask her.

"To a memory," she says, and I'm a little frustrated. We have so many memories. The cab driver almost runs over two children who are trying to cross the street. He needs to make his fare, can't afford to stop. He has a George Michael CD on. I recognize it only because Ali loves George Michael. It's the song with the saxophone, the one where he sounds so guilty. I don't really understand what he's saying. He sounds like he's pleading, and I hate that it's the song that's playing right now. Nasrin has a smile on her face while her hand stays on top of mine. She keeps her hand on mine while we sit in traffic. It feels cold. When we finally reach a parking lot, Nasrin pays the driver.

"Oh no . . ." I say as I recognize where we are. Mount Tochal. We came here with our mothers when we were five. We rode up the mountain in a rickety *télécabine,* and I clutched my mother's leg the whole time while Nasrin squealed in delight next to me. They could fit four of us inside one car because Nasrin and I were so small. I remember looking out the glass for only a moment. We were so high! In the winter the *télécabine* serves as a ski lift. In other seasons people ride just because it gives them something to do.

"Don't be scared, Sahar," Nasrin says as we walk into the park area. "They've really made great improvements. Nobody's died here in a long time." Orange juice vendors and men with gray beards tending ice-cream stations watch Nasrin as she passes by. We hop onto the shuttle with three little children with their mother. Usually the mountain is populated with couples, especially during the winter ski season. Women wear long coats and head scarves that fit snugly over their faces and hair, with goggles usually holding the scarves in place.

"Why are we doing this?" I ask. I hate heights. Nasrin knows this. She looks so relaxed as the shuttle bus ascends the mountain. She takes my hand in hers. Holding hands is a luxury couples aren't allowed in public, but we are just a pair of friends.

"The wedding is next week," she says, as though I didn't know that. As though I haven't been counting down the days and making myself sick over it.

"Is this my parting gift?" She tightens her grip on my hand. It means, "Shut up, we're in public." We don't talk again until we exit the shuttle bus and Nasrin buys two tickets to ride the *télécabine* up to the top of the mountain. The attendant in a blue jumpsuit looks at her strangely because that's a lot of money for a teenager to have for the expensive joy ride. She doesn't pay any attention as she drags me into the *télécabine* by the hand. I'm too angry to be stuck in an enclosed space with her. She doesn't give me a choice as she waits for me to enter the *télécabine*. This is the last time I will see her. I'm going to leave with Ali, and I'm not going to tell her. To hell with her . . . I don't mean that.

"Sahar, get in! Hurry," she commands.

I do mean it. She can go to hell. I get in quickly and she rushes in after me. The attendant closes the door and we ascend. The rickety, creaking noise coming from above has me terrified. I look down at the rocks and trees, which are growing smaller as we climb. We're going to fall, I'm sure of it. This is not how I expected to die. On a rickety ski lift with the girl I love and hate all at once. How will I be remembered? I can just imagine:

"You heard that Sahar Ghazvini died?"

"Who?"

"You know, Nasrin's puppy dog."

"Oh yes! The closeted lesbian who chickened out of a sex reassignment surgery, and never wore enough makeup. She was a homely thing, wasn't she?"

"So where is he taking you for your honeymoon?" I want to know. I want to pretend like I am there.

"Dubai," she mutters. She looks the antithesis of an excited bride.

"Very fancy. He can afford that, working at the transsexual clinic." She gazes out at the scenery, her jaw set. "You know how I know that. Don't pretend like you didn't know what

I was up to." I'm seething now. I expect her to look at me with those *I-have-no-idea-what-you-mean!* eyes she reserves for when she knows without a doubt she has done something wrong. I never exactly told her what I was doing, but she never asked, either. We lived within our respective delusions for far longer than this whole wedding debacle has existed.

"I didn't think that you . . . that it was something you were seriously going to do," she says.

"Does he know about us?" I ask.

"No. He didn't mention you were at the clinic. He's very earnest about his job." Of course he is. He doesn't want to compromise my patient confidentiality. I feel so embarrassed.

"Damn you, Nasrin!" I scream at her. "Damn you for doing this to me. Why would you let me fall in love with you? You knew you were never going to settle for me. Was I just something to keep you busy? A toy like the ones your parents bought for you? I hate you for leaving me behind. You were all I had after Maman . . ." She puts her arms around me and I cry into her shoulder. No, I won't let her comfort me. She doesn't deserve it.

"Sahar, look at me," she pleads. "Look at me." I look away and down the mountain. God, we're so high! I can't breathe.

We are either going to fall, or I am going to hyperventilate. She grabs me, turns my face to hers, and kisses me on the mouth. I rip myself away from her.

"What are you doing?" I look around, in back and in front of us. She steadies my face in her hands, clutching my cheeks, making me feel like a chipmunk.

"I'm kissing you in public. No one can see us up here,"

"Yeah, no one can see us up here. You're ashamed of me." She squeezes my cheeks harder.

"I'm being who you want me to be just once, and in public," she says. I kiss her forcefully. I hope her lips bruise. I hope no lipstick will be able to cover up the marks I leave. She kisses back, no hesitation, no tension or fear. I stop for breath and confirm that we have a few minutes before the next stop up the mountain. The last thing we need is for an attendant to catch us.

She tugs my hair, just like she did when we were little. "You belong to me, Sahar. I just assumed you knew that I belonged to you. I always will." She kisses me again, and I keep my eyes open to make sure we have enough time before we reach the platform. Her eyes stay closed. She really means it. I back away. I wonder if I should tell her I am thinking of going to Turkey, that I want her to come with me. She would never say yes. It would be too difficult for her to leave her life of luxury.

"I'm not waiting for you anymore, Nasrin. After the wedding we can't carry on like we have been." Her mouth gapes open in shock. She's such a petulant child.

"But just because I'm marrying him doesn't mean that we can't . . . that you can't—"

"Your husband would figure it out eventually. Then what? I won't sacrifice my life or yours for some high school love affair." I'm being intentionally cold now. We need to disconnect or she will be the death of me. I sit on my hands so I won't be tempted to touch her again.

"What is the matter with you, Sahar? Why are you being like this?" We reach a checkpoint and stop.

"Getting off or staying on?" an attendant in blue overalls asks.

"Off!" I shout, and I get out of the box as fast as I can. Cool air hits my face as I walk out to the overlook. There aren't too many people milling about, just some children with their parents. It's dusk and the lights of Tehran glow in the distance. I haven't seen the city like this since I was a child.

Everything seemed so magical then. Now the lights just seem dinky. I feel Nasrin's breath on the back of my covered neck.

"I love you," Nasrin whispers. "I will never love him the way I love you. Can't you understand that?" There is a desperate pleading in her voice, but I've heard it before. It sounds like when she was eight and begged for an overpriced dollhouse for her birthday. She had forgotten all about the dollhouse a week later.

"I understand that you want nice things," I say. "You finally want to make your parents proud of you. I know you want children to love, no matter how smart or beautiful or wretched they are. And because I know you, because I *love* you, I know that all of those things can't have anything to do with me. No matter how badly I want them to."

Nasrin starts to cry. I turn around to face her and begin crying as hard as she is. She leans in and hugs me. We cling to each other because there's nothing else left to do. We never would have reached the top of the mountain anyway.

18

ALI AND BABA STAND in the living room, their hands cupped and raised to their faces. I'm shocked to see Ali praying. That he even remembers how to do so is a miracle in itself. That my father is praying next to him in our living room makes my jaw drop. Baba hasn't prayed since Maman died. The prayers quietly leave their lips and reach the ether before the two of them drop to their knees and press their foreheads to the ground. I wait for them to finish before I clear my throat to let them know I'm awake this morning and present.

Ali turns around first and grins. "I'm a bit rusty." He chuckles and Baba pats his shoulder.

I've never been terribly religious. I believe in Allah in the same way I believe Nasrin loves me. Her love is steadfast but not always available.

"So am I," Baba says as Ali walks toward the kitchen. There's bread and cheese on the table, and tea is brewing in its pot. I've arrived in a parallel universe. Baba and I follow Ali.

"What's going on?" I ask.

"Ali is leaving," Baba says. "Tonight." I stare at Ali's profile when he pours tea into three glasses. I sit down at the table; Baba sits across from me. My appetite is nonexistent. I don't know what I'm supposed to do. If I go with Ali, it's a new start. It will be difficult, but I'll never have to be unbearably close to Nasrin again. I'll never have to see her fawn over Reza or have to face temptation any time she's feeling nostalgic and would like to take me out for a joyride, like a Honda motorcycle long neglected in Dariush's mechanic shop.

Ali puts glasses in front of Baba and me and sits down at the table. Baba takes a sip, and Ali chomps down on some bread. I inspect them both. Baba looks a little better these days. He hasn't been catatonic, and he engages in conversation with Ali every so often. Mostly it's about when Ali is planning on leaving, but even so, it's better than just watching life go by. Ali has been on his cell phone less and less this past week. I suppose his affairs have all been handled, the best they can be, anyway. They're both relaxed, leaving me the only one on edge. That's not fair.

"Why tonight?" I ask. It's so soon, and he didn't give me enough warning. I didn't agree to go, but I didn't disagree, either. Maybe the offer is rescinded.

"I've settled my finances, and I don't want to wait for Friday," Ali says in between bites. But traffic is terrible on Thursday nights. People want to get out of the city for a little break, only to spend hours in smog and dust. I'm beginning to think nothing makes sense in this country. I suppose he can't stand being in Tehran another day. Maybe I should get out. "Have any plans this evening?" Ali asks. So his offer still stands. He's leaving, never coming back, and he wants me with him. It's ludicrous, it's dangerous, and it sounds like the best offer I'm going to get.

"I don't know yet," I say. I really don't. Ali chortles and pulls out a pack of cigarettes from his pocket. He never smoked before he got in trouble with the law. Now he smokes four cigarettes a day. It reminds me of Maman and I hate that.

"I should go to school," I say as I stand up.

Baba grabs my arm gently before I can get much farther. "I

called the school and told them you were sick," he murmurs. "You and I have something to do today." Now I know I am definitely dreaming. Baba is not only pulling me out of school, he's actually spending time with me. He lets go of my arm and drinks from his glass again. "Eat something. We have a long day ahead of us."

I look at Ali, who shrugs. Even he doesn't know what Baba is up to. I spread some feta cheese crumbles on my bread and take a bite only because Baba is watching me. One bite is all I can stomach.

In the cab I figure out where we are going, after we drive past Angry Grandpa's tomb. It's a huge mosque that's bigger than the Shah's mansion, which is now a museum. The parking lot for the tomb is mostly empty, except for a cheaply made tour bus with words in Pashto written on the side. The people in the bus don't look Iranian. They're probably from Pakistan. I hate to think that this is their version of Disneyland, but everyone has a dream vacation, I guess. The cab driver takes his hands off the wheel to pray for a moment as we pass the tomb, and I hope Allah is with him so we don't crash. The driver puts his hands on the wheel again when we near the exit.

"Why are you taking me here?" I ask Baba. We haven't

been here since Maman's funeral. I didn't think we'd ever come back.

"We could use some guidance," Baba says as we enter Behesht Zahra Cemetery. Large, colorful poster art of the martyrs of the Iraq war greet us. The martyrs have a huge portion of the cemetery for themselves. The place is huge because this is where all of Tehran's dead go. It's as large as several football stadiums and just as well kept. Baba tells the driver what numbered section Maman's grave is in, and the driver follows the signs. The dusty roads are lined with trees as far as the eye can see. I remember thinking that on the day of the funeral, too.

Baba tells the driver to stop and pays him. The driver says a little prayer again; it's becoming tiresome. I get out of the car and think about all the cab fare Baba has wasted to get us here. We could have saved that money for something important. There's a little girl, no more than six or seven, selling flowers out of a small bucket. Baba walks to her and buys one flower for each of us. He also buys a bottle of water from her to wash the grave. It has probably gathered a lot of dirt.

We both begin walking onto the field of graves. All the tiles, the graves, are squeezed so close together that it's impossible not to walk on some of them. Some graves have photographs of the dead on top of the tombstones. I remember Maman's is near one that has a photograph of a fat mustached man wearing a hat. He looks so confused in the photograph. I can't imagine it's the best photograph that his family could find to commemorate him. When I finally see it, my throat tightens, and I can hear Baba doing his best not to cry, too.

We look down at Maman's grave. Baba unscrews the bottle of water and washes away the dust on the headstone, revealing curved, engraved words in Farsi telling the world that she was a beloved wife and mother. We both just stare at the script. I wish we had had more money to make the calligraphy slightly fancier. Isn't that a strange thing to think?

Baba crouches down and puts one hand on the grave. He looks up at me and expects me to do the same. I don't know why. Praying isn't going to make her rest any easier, but it's a custom, and so I crouch down until my palm lays flat and heavy on the word *mother*. Baba whispers the prayer, and I stay silent. She wouldn't like that I skipped school to do this. She would tell me that studying her grave isn't going to get me into university and then groan at Baba's maudlin behavior. Then she'd probably hold his hand and tell him not to worry me so much. Baba stands back up and I follow suit. We place the pink carnations on her grave.

"*Salam,* Hayedeh," Baba says. "I apologize for not coming sooner. It was difficult to . . . well, I wasn't ready." This is just too strange. "Look at our daughter. Isn't she beautiful?"

"Baba, stop," I plead with him. "She can't hear you." He nods and takes a deep breath. I don't think he was buying it, either. It was a valiant try, though. He looks me square in the eyes, and I see him as he was before Maman died.

"She would be proud of you, your work at school and taking care of me. You've turned into a wonderful young woman. I don't know how much credit I can take for that, but you have, and I'm so grateful to her spirit for watching over you." Don't cry, Sahar. Be strong for him, otherwise he is going to start bawling. "She'd also want you to be happy. She'd want both of us to be happy. And we haven't been, have we?" I could lie. We have had happy moments. Separate from each other and not nearly as many as we used to, but we're not so sad are we? We're not so terribly tragic that he looks like an old man and I tried to become a man . . .

"No, Baba. No, we haven't been."

Baba takes in my answer and stares down at the grave. "Are you going to leave?" he asks. "With Ali?" There isn't any emotion in his voice when he asks. I wonder if Ali told him he asked me to go to Turkey with him. It doesn't matter. He knows now.

"It's tempting," I say. "Having a place to start over." God, what's wrong with me? I'm not denying it or sparing his feelings. I'm a bad daughter. Baba starts crying now. I'm on the verge of tears myself.

"Is it so bad here? Have I been that . . . that despondent?"

Yes, you have. But I still love you.

"You haven't done anything wrong." He's still crying as he reaches for my hand. I take his in mine and we both stare at the grave, hoping she'll come out from under there and tell us to stop being such babies.

"Please stay, Sahar. For me."

"I'm scared of what the future holds for me. And now that Nasrin is getting married, I will be facing that future alone. That terrifies me."

"You'll be leaving me to face *my* future alone, Sahar. I know I don't deserve it, but if you stay, I'll be better—I promise. You won't have to cook anymore, and we can go for walks in the park like we used to." He hasn't been this passionate about something in years. The calligraphy on the grave becomes blurry, as I can no longer suppress my tears. "And what about your dream of being a doctor? You're going to give that all up because life is difficult? Life is difficult everywhere!" He's channeling Maman now. It's about time. He's being a real parent, and that makes me cry even harder.

"You just don't want to be alone," I manage to say between sobs. "You don't care about my happiness." He tightens his grip on my hand. I can feel him staring at me.

"Your happiness is important to me, but yes, I'm asking you selfishly. I'm sorry if I . . . if I don't always show it that I care. It's difficult to know what you are thinking. Your mother was like that. I had to dig to find out what was troubling her. I'm sorry if I haven't tried as hard with you."

You wouldn't want to know what is happening in my life. You would be disappointed with me. Maybe even disgusted, and I could not handle that because you will be all the family I have left.

"If I stay you won't ever leave me again, will you, Baba? You promise you won't act like a walking ghost anymore? Because I'm tired of it, and she would be, too." He nods and I hug him. He wraps his wiry arms around me. He is so frail, but it feels like he's growing stronger and surer the longer he holds me. I'm almost tempted to tell him I have missed him.

Ali and Parveen are sitting in the living room when we return. Parveen is crying and Ali just continues to watch the television. It's a Brazilian soap opera, dubbed in Farsi, that's showing on an illegal channel from the West.

"Did the doctor find out she was faking her pregnancy?" Baba asks, and I look at him in shock. I wasn't aware he was a soap enthusiast.

"No. I think he's still trying to give her the benefit of the doubt," Ali says, stubbing out a cigarette in the Saddam Hussein ashtray. Parveen keeps crying, even while she gives my father a polite smile.

"Can I get you anything, Parveen *khanum*?" Baba asks. I'm pretty sure Baba doesn't know Parveen is a transsexual, but I like to think that even if he did know he wouldn't treat her differently.

"No. I'm sorry. I'm just . . . I'm upset about the situation and . . ." She keeps whimpering, and Ali rolls his eyes.

"I told her she could always visit me. I'm not dying, just

relocating." He sounds exasperated. And he's jittery, bouncing one knee up and down and immediately lighting another cigarette. "Sahar, what did you decide?" He never was one to beat around the bush. Sometimes I wish more people were like that.

"When Parveen visits you, so will I," I say, and I can hear all the tension leave Baba in one deep breath. Ali looks annoyed but not surprised. I think he is getting used to not being able to call the shots any longer.

"Suit yourself. It's a shame, though. I could have used a partner." Ali says. He is a social person and doesn't do well alone. I think it might kill him not to have someone to boss around. Parveen blows her nose into a tissue loudly, and it's the most unlady-like thing I have ever seen her do. We're all just waiting for Mother and Daughter to show up to pick up Ali.

"Sahar, may I speak to you in your room for a moment?" Ali asks, and I nod. He leads the way and then closes the door to my bedroom behind me. "Are you sure you want to stay? I can wait if you need more time to think about it." We both know he can't wait. He's lucky he has managed to go unharmed for this long since the police incident.

"I'm an Iranian, Ali. No matter what else I am, this is home."

He scoffs at my newfound patriotism, though he knows it isn't quite that. It's the situation. He knows Iran is his home, too, even if he doesn't want it to be.

"I'll send you photographs of Turkish women." He grins. "You'll change your mind in no time."

I don't know who else I will be able to have conversations like this with. "I'm going to miss you."

"Naturally," he says with a hip check. That's his way of saying he will miss me, too. "You're going to be able to handle the wedding without me?" No. I won't.

"I'll be okay. I think. Baba's not such a terrible date. He never talks my ear off like you do." We both laugh at that. The buzzer sounds to signal that Ali's ride has arrived. He kisses me on my cheek.

"I'll let you know where to write me, once I get settled." I nod, and we go back down the hall to rejoin the others. Ali opens the front door to reveal Mother, looking especially irritated, and Daughter, who has a new bruise on her face.

"Take her with you," I whisper into Ali's ear. If he's so eager to have a companion, let it be someone who really deserves a second chance. He smiles at me and begins to make his good-byes. He shakes Baba's hand and Baba actually hugs him. Parveen cries and kisses both of his cheeks. She then holds a Koran in the air for Ali to walk under three times, to assure him safe passage. It's comical because Ali has to duck down and waddle underneath. When he straightens up, he hugs Parveen. Ali is crying now, and I have to stare at the floor because his crying makes me so uncomfortable. *Ali doesn't cry.*

I look back at Nastaran and give her a small smile. She waves at me. Ali picks up his backpack and grabs the handle of his roller suitcase. It's all he needs to carry. He leaves the apartment abruptly, before anyone can convince him to stay. Mother rolls her eyes and grabs Nastaran by the arm, dragging her out of the apartment. When I shut the door Parveen drops down on the couch, crying into her hands. Baba doesn't know what to do but brew some tea. I'm proud that he actually does it himself. I lean against the door, trying to process what Ali's departure signifies.

"He's going to be fine, isn't he?" Parveen asks in between sobs. I nod. He always is. My cell phone beeps and I have an SMS message. It's probably an advertisement to remind us to pray for an imam who died hundreds of years ago. I welcome any kind of distraction as I open my phone to read it: *Keep dreaming, kiddo. Check under your bed.*

Of course Ali has to be cryptic until the last minute. I hope he hasn't left me any gay-man pornography or opium. I go into my room and lie on my belly to reach under my bed. It's a medium-sized Adidas sports bag, and I'm almost afraid to open it. Oh, please don't be something illegal. My whole body shakes as I unzip the bag. It's full of money, and that devil gets me crying again.

19

THE HAIR SALON SMELLS of hairspray, nail polish remover, and sugar. This combination is the smell I will always associate with disappointment. Mrs. Mehdi continues to hover over Nasrin's chair as the stressed makeup artist tries to accommodate both Nasrin and her mother, which is almost impossible. Nasrin insists she needs more eyeliner, and Mrs. Mehdi tells her that more will make her look like a whore. I look at my reflection while my hairstylist loudly disapproves of how dry my hair is. I would like to punch her, but I just don't have the energy. I've taken one of Baba's new antidepressants to stop the sick feeling in my stomach. I hope he doesn't notice, but I'm willing to risk it today. Reza should be here any minute to pick up his bride in the Mercedes he's rented for the occasion, and Nasrin is getting more and more agitated.

"Hold still, Nasrin!" Mrs. Mehdi snaps. Nasrin huffs on the brink of a tantrum. They've been at each other's throats for two hours. The other women in the salon try to make polite conversation over the blow dryers, but the tension is thick. Two of Nasrin's friends from school are here. I've seen them at birthday parties and on excursions to the mall, but I think Nasrin views them as filler friends, the kind to waste time with. Mrs. Mehdi's sister-in-law and a cousin are also on hand as the other special, overly made-up hussies of the day. They both always look at me like I'm a poor, helpless orphan. I hate them.

"If you add any more eye shadow, then I *will* look like a prostitute," Nasrin barks. "Is that what you want? He's already spending enough money on me. I think people will get the message without all this gold on my eyelids." I know this is hard on her. Mrs. Mehdi pinches her daughter's waist, and Nasrin lifts a little out of her chair. I think Mrs. Mehdi would have slapped her if doing so wouldn't have ruined Nasrin's makeup.

"I think I'd better change into my dress," I mutter to get my hairstylist off my case about which conditioner I should be using.

"That's a great idea, Sahar!" Nasrin says as she jumps out of her seat. "I'll join you."

Mrs. Mehdi is fuming. "Why don't you wait for Sahar to change first?"

Nasrin gives her mother a look that could freeze the desert. "I need help with my dress," she hisses, and drags me into the back room where all the ladies' dresses are hanging. She locks the door behind us and rubs her temples, groaning. "At least after today she can't boss me around anymore." I touch her face softly and she leans into my hand.

"I'm not smudging your makeup, am I?" I ask, genuinely worried that Mrs. Mehdi might have a conniption.

"I don't care," she whispers, and kisses my palm. "Let's get this over with." I imagine she will say the same thing to Reza tonight when he wants to be intimate. What a fruitful marriage. She begins to undress and I soak in every curve, every part of her that she sees as a flaw and I see as a revelation.

"Stop staring, Sahar. You're making me blush, and that might throw off my stupid color scheme." She chuckles, but I don't feel like laughing. She steps into the dress that she has carelessly taken from the garment rack, pulls it up, and asks me to zip her in.

I inch closer to her and reach down to pull up the zipper.

My hands caress her exposed shoulders. I can feel her goose bumps pebble under my fingertips. "Are you nervous?"

"I'll just be glad when the day is through. All I want are excellent photographs and to dance near you." She turns around to face me. She's the bride I always wanted. "Put on your dress," she whispers, and I comply. Parveen helped me pick the sleek black sheath. That was my only criteria for my garb, that it be black. Nasrin looks me over and takes my hands. "Let's pretend. Like we used to."

When we were little, we would pretend to marry each other. Usually one of Nasrin's stuffed animals would fill the role of the mullah, and the Barbie dolls would be our witnesses. "You look so beautiful," Nasrin tells me.

"So do you," I murmur. "You're the wife of my dreams." I kiss her cheek, and then I clear my throat, because we have to go. "We're not six anymore, Nasrin. There's no more time for pretend." Being a grown-up is stupid, though. It's stupid but necessary, and if this is what she really wants for us, I can't do anything to stop it.

Nasrin fans her eyes so she doesn't start crying and ruin her mascara. "I'm sorry that . . . Well, you know, about all of this. I just don't see how . . ."

"Fine. It's fine." It isn't, but I don't see an alternative. "He's a lucky man and . . . Be happy. That's what I want for you." I open the door after that because I feel suffocated and can't stand to look at her without wanting to kiss her — or smash her face. Keep calm. The day hasn't even really started yet.

All the women in the salon cheer for Nasrin in her dress.

"Nasrin, hurry!" Mrs. Mehdi shouts. "Reza's car is outside!" Nasrin rolls her eyes but smiles at all the attention she is getting. Her two friends from high school wrap a bridal shawl around her head and torso so she can walk in public. Then she leaves. The other women and I look out from the door, all of us smooshed together so we can see Reza's rental car, with orange flower garlands all over. Reza greets Nasrin and helps her into the car, checking and rechecking to make sure that all of her dress is fitting in the front seat. His face is pale and shiny from sweat. I back away from the crowd by the door and find my coat and head scarf. The other cars to take the rest of us to the ceremony will be here shortly, and I can't look at the happy couple much longer, anyway.

Mrs. Mehdi reenters the salon with her head scarf so loosely draped she might as well not be wearing one. "Ladies!

Get ready—our rides are here." The women scramble to find their coats, scarves and bags; to touch up whatever makeup they can; and to make final assessments of themselves in mirrors. Mrs. Mehdi walks to me and takes my hand. "You'll ride with me," she says. It's not an invitation.

We rush outside, and Cyrus opens the door of the Mehdis' Benz for me. I enter the car, sliding across the backseat to make room for the queen. As soon as she enters, the car fills with perfume, a designer scent that reeks of wealth. The dutiful son closes the door behind her, and then takes command of the steering wheel. Mrs. Mehdi and I both sit there in the backseat, neither of us speaking to the other. Cyrus begins to drive, his mother complaining that he is going too fast or too slow until the poor guy looks almost as bad as Reza did. Mrs. Mehdi puts her hand over mine in the middle of the seat.

"It's over now. You understand?" I look at her and she doesn't make eye contact; she keeps her eyes on the road to make sure Cyrus doesn't crash into anything. I could pretend I don't know what she is talking about. But after today it doesn't really matter anymore.

"I understand. Perfectly," I say, and she lets go of my hand. I look out the window at the traffic on the autobahn. I try to focus on details. We pass a vendor selling corn on the side of the road, two motorcyclists without helmets, and rows of Iranian flags aligned straight on exit ramps. "You must be very happy today," I tell her, still looking out the window. "Reza is a handsome groom."

"Enough."

"I'm just saying my congratulations! Such a wonderful marriage you've planned, right, Cyrus?" I'm angry, but Cyrus is too dim to pick up on it. He just smiles, nods, and honks at the car in front of him. "She'll be taken care of. She'll never have to do anything for herself or explore the world. A housewife, just like you! What a lucky darling."

"Not everyone is as clever as you are, Sahar," she says. "Or as troubled." I almost want to lunge at her and scratch her face with my newly manicured nails.

"No, Nasrin is a good girl. A very, *very* good girl." And yes, I meant the comment to sound perverse, even though it embarrasses me to even entertain the thought of Nasrin having sex. Mrs. Mehdi's hand is on mine again, this time with a bone-crushing grip. We make eye contact, and we both know we'll never speak of this moment again. We probably won't speak about anything again.

"This is the best thing," she whispers. "For the *both* of you." I know that one day I will agree with her. There is no way Nasrin and I can ever really be together. We all know that. I deflate and lean back against the leather seat. Mrs. Mehdi eases her grip but keeps her hand on mine the rest of the way to the ceremony. Her hand trembles a little. She's scared, too. Of me, I think.

We at last arrive at the villa Nasrin's grandfather owns. There are so many cars, and so many people walking to the wedding. It looks more like a funeral.

"Cyrus, go inside and make sure your father isn't drunk already," Mrs. Mehdi says. "It's only two in the afternoon." Cyrus rushes out of the car. We're alone now.

"I'm not going to say anything in there," I mutter. "I know she has to do this. You haven't given her much choice." Mrs. Mehdi takes her hand off mine. I ball my own hand into a fist.

"You are so like your mother," she says. "She lost everything to be with your *baba*. Her wealth, status, family — and she never looked back." Don't cry. Don't let her see you cry. "I admit that my husband and I aren't madly in love. I used to wonder what it would be like, to be in love with someone. But after the children and the memories we shared, I don't think about that anymore. You see? It goes away."

No. I don't think it does go away. I know it won't for me. I will keep busy. I will distract myself. I will eventually have days when I don't have to remind myself to breathe. I know Nasrin will exist, maybe even be happy, and I will be okay. I'll bury my love, but it will never really go away.

Mrs. Mehdi shakes her head and looks at a group of her in-laws, their big, bouffant hairstyles shrouded by ostentatious Versace head scarves. "Look at them. So much money, and they still don't know what to do with it."

"How long have you known?" I ask. I don't know why. It doesn't matter anymore.

"I suppose I pretended not to know for a great many years. I thought that I was imagining things. But she looks at you the way I wish someone had looked at me. Just once." Mrs. Mehdi smiles sadly. I don't know whether to strangle her or to give her a hug because she's the closest connection to my *maman* that I have. "I had to marry her off. You understand? Because if I could see it, it would only be a matter of time before someone else did." She begins to tremble. Fear dominates everything.

I step out of the car. I take deep breaths, hold my stomach, and silence any thoughts about screaming. And so I go forward. Shoulders back, like a good soldier, and I walk into the parlor, where chubby women dressed far too young for their ages hand their coats to a servant, their perfumes mingling in an odor I will always associate with sadness.

I take off my head scarf and coat, hanging them myself in the open closet by the door. I smooth out my dress and let myself be ushered into a living room, where the bride and groom sit next to each other. Reza looks so sure, so proud, even though he bounces his leg up and down. Nasrin puts a hand on his knee to stop him. She's always in control.

The *sofra,* a large ceremonial cloth, is spread on the floor before them, laden with all the traditional wedding flourishes: a rainbow of flowers, an open Koran, colored walnuts arranged in beautiful designs, lit candles on either side of a golden-rimmed mirror that the bride and groom can see themselves in. It's all too much to take in. I'm desperate to look at something, *anything,* else.

I look at Mr. Mehdi, who, after speaking with the mullah, has paid a group connected to the regime to allow the wedding to be coed. I look at Cyrus, who keeps checking his watch. I look at Dariush, standing next to Cyrus with a grin on his face that confirms to me that he and Sima have had sex. The other close friends and family push from behind me to crowd into the room. One of Nasrin's filler friends, giddy and idiotic, grabs my hand and pulls me behind the couple. The friends and a few of Nasrin's female cousins hold a linen cloth above the couple's heads. I don't dare look down to see the couple's reflection in the mirror.

Everyone is quiet now and the mullah begins. One of Nasrin's cousins to my left hands me the two corncob-sized blocks of sugar draped in white mesh, which I am to grind over the linen, ensuring the couple a sweet marriage. I begin to grind lightly, listening to the mullah go on about what marriage means and how pleased Allah would be at the union of these two fine people, whom the mullah has probably met only twenty minutes ago.

The mullah asks Nasrin if she accepts Reza as her husband. One friend calls, "The bride has gone to pick flowers!" Many people find this tradition cute and coy, but it sickens me now. The mullah asks Nasrin again, and one of her cousins says, "The bride has gone to put the flowers in a vase!" I grind the sugar feverishly. There will soon be no sugar left to grind, if I keep up this pace.

The mullah asks Nasrin one more time if she accepts Reza as her husband. I can't help but look at the reflection in the mirror to see Nasrin looking back at me. She smiles, genuinely, probably for the last time today.

Say something. End this. It's a lie. Everything about this is a lie.

I nod, and let her go. She looks at the ground, and gives her answer.

"With the permission of my parents and elders, I accept." All the women cheer, yelping and making noises like Indians in cowboy movies. All that is left is to ask Reza. I am grinding the sugar violently, with more focus than I think anyone has ever devoted to this stupid tradition.

"*Baleh!* Yes!" Reza says, and the whole room erupts in cheers. I open my mouth, but no sound comes out. The mullah has them sign their marriage certificate. Afterward they dip their pinkies in a glass of honey and feed each other. I hope I'm not visibly cringing. My stomach feels like it's caving in. Everything hurts. Nasrin pulls her pinky from his mouth with a smile. Mrs. Mehdi is dabbing her eyes. Tears of joy or guilt? I'm not quite certain. Mr. Mehdi slaps his son on the back. Reza's parents approach the *sofra,* showing all the gifts they now bestow upon the couple. They are followed by aunts, uncles, and grandparents, who proffer pieces of jewelry, and at last by Mr. Mehdi, who presents a deed to a villa so expensive that Nasrin starts crying.

So do I.

Nasrin's stupid cousin next to me pats my shoulder. "Isn't it wonderful?" she asks, and I nod, wiping my eyes. The bride and groom stand and then exit, to have their photographs taken. I watch Nasrin walk away, on Reza's arm, and she doesn't look back. Not once. She'll be happy. She'll be taken care of. She'll never have to worry about me.

We are free of each other.

"Sahar? Are you all right?" Baba asks me. I snap out of my daze. He looks at me with a worried expression. All the others have made their way to the courtyard in back.

"Yes. I'm sorry," I whisper. "I guess I just don't believe it. She's married."

Baba smiles and offers me his arm. "You girls are growing up so fast. One day it will be your wedding, *Insha 'Allah,*" he says. The poor man—he is always so clueless. Right now

I love him for it. I take his arm and ready myself for all the dancing, the pleasantries, and the vomit-inducing kisses the happy couple will share.

"Let's go," I say, and together we venture into the worst night of my life.

20

"Pencils down," Professor Aminzadeh says. I was one question away from finishing my biology midterm. University is more difficult than I thought it would be, but I'm grateful for the challenge. It's kept my thoughts occupied. When I saw my name in the newspaper as one of the accepted students to Tehran University a few weeks after the wedding, I didn't laugh or yell or call Baba. I just sighed and thanked god that I had something to keep me busy. The Concours was hell, but so was watching Nasrin get married.

I pass my test to the front, to the professor's assistant collecting them, and I look at Taraneh. She shrugs sheepishly, and I laugh as I stand up. We meet outside the classroom.

"I didn't get to the last question," I say.

"Last question?" Taraneh raises an eyebrow. "I think I got half of that exam wrong! I'm never going to pass."

Taraneh is a good student. Not as good as me, but studying is all I have to do. She comes from Shiraz and lives in the female dormitory. I live at home, with Baba. We bonded in Professor Aminzadeh's class, groaning over our lecture notes and commiserating about his illegible handwriting. She's part of my study group. We're a serious bunch of five girls, but sometimes we go to the movies or smoke a hookah together at a teahouse. Taraneh and I are the only ones in our group without boyfriends, but we never talk about it. I don't mind the boys. Soheila's boyfriend is funny and never takes his studies all that seriously. He reminds me of Ali.

I hear from Ali, but I can't write him, because he never includes a return address on the envelopes for the letters he sends. I think he will let me know how to reach him. He says he's doing okay in Istanbul, working as a nightclub promoter. I have a feeling that he hands out flyers and hangs around hotels to entice tourists to come with him.

He and Nastaran pretend to be brother and sister. She keeps their shoe-box apartment clean. In one photograph Ali sent, he and Nastaran are on either side of an obese Israeli drag queen named Big Sara. Nastaran sticks her tongue out at the camera, and the drag queen swoons while Ali kisses him on the cheek. I taped it onto my bedroom wall. It makes me smile every time I look at it.

"What are you doing tomorrow?" Taraneh asks. Tomorrow is Thursday. After class I will cook dinner and study, and Parveen will come over and we will have tea. She will discuss her fresh crush on Jamshid from group, and I will chuckle halfheartedly. Goli *khanum* has noticed Parveen's crush, so she often asks Parveen and Jamshid to prepare the tea for everyone in the kitchen. The blooming romance has also distracted the group from Maryam's absence. She's back on the street, selling herself for drug money.

After Parveen leaves I will study some more. Baba will come home from his workshop, and we will eat dinner together. Ali left behind so much money that Baba was able to rent a better work space and to hire an assistant. His business has been growing, and I can actually see glimpses of his life before Maman passed away. After dinner we will talk about the day. Then we will watch the newest soap opera from Brazil, dubbed in Farsi. Baba will yell at the television, hoping "Julianna" will somehow hear him and run away with Dr. Claudio.

"I'm not doing much," I tell Taraneh as we exit onto the quad. "I have a lot of studying to do." There are some young men playing football. Badly. Students huddle around the juice stand, sipping on melon drinks while checking their cell phones. Two young women are selling tickets to a campus concert featuring the poetry of Hafiz.

"If you want to take a break, maybe we can hang out?" Taraneh suggests.

"Oh, is the group up to something?"

"No." Taraneh smiles shyly at me. "I just thought maybe you and I could do something. Alone." I stop in my tracks and look at Taraneh. She has my undivided attention at last as she continues. "I was thinking of checking out Restaurant Javan. Have you heard of it?"

Oh. She's clutching her backpack strap tight, probably in response to my gaping mouth.

"Yes, I have been there before," I say. "Have you?" She bites her lip and nods. I close my mouth and gulp. "Well, I'm . . . I'm glad that you have been there, too. It's a nice place. I, um . . . I just don't think I am ready to go back there yet."

"The food isn't that great?" she asks, arching one perfectly tweezed eyebrow. I laugh a little. She's funny. I never noticed.

"How did you, um . . . how did you know about me?" I ask, hoping I am not obvious.

"I wasn't completely sure. Just hopeful. Plus, you never appreciate Dr. Claudio when he appears on television. Objectively, he's a very attractive man." She says it so easily—like we are talking about the most normal thing in the world.

"I don't know that I'm necessarily ready for a new dinner companion at Restaurant Javan," I admit.

She smiles at me. "I was heartbroken once."

God, I'm so obvious. She touches my sneaker with hers in solidarity.

"Sahar!" I turn around to find Reza, standing by his double-parked Mercedes. He looks tired, confused, and even scared. I tremble at the sight of him.

"Who is that?" Taraneh asks. I should just say he's nobody and continue walking with her. I've done my best to forget about all of it these past six months. I haven't spoken to Nasrin since the wedding. "Do you want me to stay with you?" Taraneh offers, nervous for my safety. I'm surprised that I never noticed any special attention from her before now. I'll have to ask another time how she got over her broken heart. I kiss both of her cheeks, say good-bye, and walk over to Reza.

"Sahar, I am sorry to bother you. I know you're busy with school but I — it's Nasrin,"

"Is she hurt? Is she okay?" I'm panicking now. She's too selfish to harm herself. Isn't she?

"She's not hurt. But she . . . She's been crying a lot, and I don't know what's bothering her. She won't tell me. We were doing fine until a week ago. I don't know how to get her to open up." Maybe what she's done is at last catching up with her. "Will you please come see her?"

No. It's over. He's supposed to take care of her now. He's her better half. I'm nothing to her anymore. It isn't a good idea.

"Please," he says. "You're her best friend." Everything comes flooding back. All of our birthdays; all of our New Year's celebrations; Maman's hospital room; watching Nasrin dance, tutoring her in math, her hugging me when the world felt overwhelming. She has been there for all of it.

"Let's go," I say, and Reza rushes to the front passenger seat door, opening it for me. He quickly gets into the driver's seat and peels out onto the street, almost colliding with two taxis. This type of driving is typical in Tehran, but I've never before seen it from Reza.

"Stupid traffic!" He pounds on his horn as soon as he merges onto the highway. His radio plays classical Iranian music.

"Nasrin hates classical music," I tell him. He looks over at me in confusion.

"She told me she loves it." Of course she did.

"She lied to you." I'd like to tell him about all the other things she has lied about. He's gripping the steering wheel tighter now and scrutinizes me as we sit in traffic. I stare back at him, waiting for him to ask. He can't hurt me anymore.

"Why were you at the clinic?" he asks, like he doesn't know. Does he want confirmation of all the thoughts he's been trying to keep at bay? Do I want to give him that satisfaction?

The traffic is finally moving. A watermelon truck is now in the breakdown lane, and green globes of various sizes are strewn across the exit ramp. I bite the inside of my cheek to keep in all the things I want to say like, "I know you're nice but I can't stand you," or "Your wife is totally hot for me, you dumb donkey."

"It doesn't matter now." You won, Reza. I lost. Game over. He accelerates and merges onto the next exit, the one that leads to all the fancy villas with large, ornate iron gates.

"I love Nasrin," he says. "I'm committed to her, even when her behavior is sometimes . . . irrational. I know she had a life before me, and I'd rather not know what that entailed." He gulps. His uncertainty gives me no satisfaction.

We approach the villa gate and he opens it with a remote. The high life — their villa looks like a prison. A gorgeous, large, glamorous prison with a princess trapped inside. He puts the car in park. Then he just sits there, tapping his fingers on the steering wheel. The gallant prince has yet to get off his steed to save the day. "I hate that I can't comfort her or make her happy all the time." I really hope he doesn't start bawling, or this is going to be exceedingly uncomfortable.

"Nothing's ever perfect," I murmur. "Especially with Nasrin." He chortles at that, and I guess he's figured out how spoiled Nasrin can be. Especially when she wants something she can't have anymore.

"She misses her best friend. You know her better than anyone else. Maybe you know her even better than she knows herself. And so I hope that when I invite you into our home, you will act accordingly." The prince isn't here to save the princess. He's gone and recruited the court jester to do the job. I nod as he unbuckles his seat belt and opens his door. I don't wait for him to open mine, even though he's rushing around the car to do so.

I look up at the ornate house. It's not as nice as the Mehdis', but it's pretty close. I'm ready to climb the castle walls. Reza leads me inside. The marble floors probably cost more than fifteen years' rent at Baba's workshop.

"She's in our bedroom," Reza says. We both walk up the marble stairs. It's a little much, even for Nasrin. We reach a rich mahogany door, and Reza knocks on it quietly. *"Azizam,* it's me. Can you let me in?" No answer. Reza leans his head against the door and sighs. I imagine he has been doing this for a very long time. I put my hand on his shoulder and gently try to pull him away. He backs away from the door and walks down the hallway, out of sight.

"Nasrin?" I call to her gently. "Reza tells me you haven't talked to him for a few days. He's worried about you. I'm here now. Let me in. *Please.*"

She opens the door, and she has tears smearing her cheeks. It must be bad. She isn't wearing any makeup. She walks back to her bed and curls into a fetal position, making herself very small and turning her back to me. The lights are off, and crumpled tissues are strewn all over her nightstand.

"What are you doing here?" she mumbles.

"Reza. He brought me."

"He fetched you to fix me? How stupid of him." She says that last bit in disbelief. I don't blame her. I sit on the edge of the bed, looking down at her curled-up form. Seeing her so helpless makes me sick to my stomach. "I haven't seen you in months," she says. It was something we had decided together. It would make the change easier, for both of us. "Did you miss me?" Her voice sounds desperate. I lie down next to her and hold her in my arms, her back against my chest, her frayed and unkempt hair brushing my face.

"I miss you every moment of every day, you spoiled brat."

She makes a noise that I think is a laugh. I will accept any noise she is willing to utter.

"Does it go away?" she asks. "Missing each other?"

I think about how much I missed Maman. I still do, though it isn't as acute as it once was. "A little bit," I whisper. "Enough so that life continues. In a year you won't even think about me." She turns around in my arms and looks up at me, tugging at a strand of my hair.

"Don't say stupid things, Sahar. You're smarter than that." She curls my hair around one finger and unravels it just as quickly. Don't kiss her. Those days are over. She's your friend now. Be her friend.

"I'm pregnant." She starts crying. I hold still for a moment, making absolutely sure I don't cringe or vomit.

"Does Reza know?" I ask shakily. She shakes her head no. He's going to be thrilled and she's not ready for that. "Isn't this what you wanted? A family of your own?" She starts sobbing now, guttural sobs that make her whole body quake. I try to soothe her the best I can by holding her close and patting her hair. Eventually she calms enough to get words out.

"When the doctor told me, I wished you were there with me. I love this baby already, whether it's a boy or a girl, but he or she won't know what you mean to me. The best person I know won't be around anymore. And suddenly everything seemed like a huge mistake. You're the one I should grow old with. And I can't."

We're both crying now. My tears roll down, quickly and quietly—no sobs. She always has to outshine me in the dramatics department.

She is in this now, and there is no way Reza will ever let her take the baby away from him. If they divorced, custody would go to him. I am not worth that. I would feel guilt for the rest of my life, and anyway, Nasrin would never give up her child.

I hope it's a girl. God, she'll be beautiful.

I wipe my tears with one hand and pull away from Nasrin. She will be fine once the baby arrives, the love for her child overshadowing anything else. I have to be the strong one. Just like when we were kids.

"You're always going to be a part of me, Nasrin." She tries to catch her breath between gasps and stares at me with longing. I shake my head. "Not like we were, but it can be enough. It *has* to be enough." I don't flinch, I don't stammer, I don't feel I am saying the wrong thing. It doesn't matter anymore. *I* shouldn't matter anymore.

Nasrin frowns. I smile a little and tell her, "You're looking at me the way I looked at you." She grimaces when she hears *looked,* past tense. I pretend that I don't notice, for both our sakes.

"I'm sorry," she says. So she has finally apologized. It's not as satisfying as I thought it would be.

I take her hand in mine. "Don't be," I say. "I'm looking forward to being an aunt. Under Reza's supervision, anyway."

She laughs. We both know he'll do whatever she wants, and I'll be able to visit them whenever I please. She stares at our hands clasped together. I would hold her hand forever if I could.

But I can't. So I let go. I love her, and I have to let go.

Acknowledgments

Chris Lynch for being the Mr. Miyagi to my Daniel-san and believing in me; Elise Howard for changing my life and being a generally awesome human being; Chris Crutcher, Tony Abbott, Amy Downing for being so generous; my agent Leigh Feldman at Writer's House and Ken Wright for introducing us; Emily Parliman and Jean Garnett for all of their work; Algonquin Books for taking on this story; Lesley University's MFA program; every teacher I have ever had (even the math teachers); and my friends and family.